Her ~~heart began~~ ~~...~~ **...** **her throat. Her skin had come alive at his touch, tingling and yearning for more.**

He's going to kiss me!

And she realised she wanted him to. Wanted it more than anything else in the whole wide world!

She sat up slightly and met him halfway, wrapping her hand behind his neck, embedding her fingers in his tousled hair and pulling his face towards hers, meeting his lips with hers, indulging in a wonderful, tentative, exploring first kiss.

Fireworks were going off throughout her body. She felt tense and relaxed and excited all at once. Her hands itched for his touch, to be holding him. Their mouths opened as the kiss deepened and his tongue took hers, and then she was breathing him, kissing him, holding him, in a way she'd never felt with a man before. His bristles scorched her face and it was a sweet agony as passion took them both by surprise and hunger for each other burned them to their very core.

This is Lucas!

Of course it was! He'd been there in front of her all this time, the man for her, and she'd let him be just a friend for all that time—not knowing, never allowing herself to think about it. *Why* hadn't she thought about it?

Perhaps I did. In fact I know I did!

She'd once let the thought of what it would be like to sleep with Lucas occupy her mind for many a night. But she'd not wanted to risk their friendship. She'd always dismissed it.

I need to breathe.

She couldn't remember how. Instead she continued to kiss him, to feel his soft hair in her fingers, his chest against hers, the yearning for more...

For so long she'd ~~...~~ ~~...would be like~~. This moment. This kiss. ~~...~~ ~~...~~ t him go. Bec~~...~~

'We sh~~...~~ k it... there's ~~...~~

Dear Reader

Hello, and welcome to my very first Mills and Boon® Medical Romance™! I wanted to kick off my medical writing career exploring an issue that has always fascinated me, and so I knew I *had* to do a surrogacy story.

I'm nowhere near brave enough to be a surrogate myself, but I am eternally fascinated and proud of those women who do volunteer to have a baby for someone else. In this story that woman is Callie Taylor—a midwife, a fascinating woman who loves babies but has never wanted one for herself. Or so she thinks...

It led me to thinking: just what happens when the surrogate has doubts about what she's doing? When I heard about women who'd ended up keeping the baby I knew I had to explore this with my characters, Callie and Lucas. They both deserve love and I hope you will enjoy their journey as much as I enjoyed writing about it.

I would love to hear from readers. If you want to contact me you can do so at Twitter, on @louisaheaton, on Facebook at www.Facebook.com/Louisaheatonauthor, or on my website: www.louisaheaton.com

Warmest wishes

Louisa

THE BABY
THAT CHANGED
HER LIFE

BY
LOUISA HEATON

Published in Great Britain 2015
by Mills & Boon, an imprint of Harlequin (UK) Limited,
Eton House, 18-24 Paradise Road, Richmond, Surrey, TW9 1SR

© 2015 Louisa Heaton

ISBN: 978-0-263-24684-1

Harlequin (UK) Limited's policy is to use papers that are natural,
renewable and recyclable products and made from wood grown in
sustainable forests. The logging and manufacturing processes conform
to the legal environmental regulations of the country of origin.

Printed and bound in Spain
by Blackprint CPI, Barcelona

Louisa Heaton first started writing romance at secondary school, and would take her stories in to show her friends, scrawled on lined A4 paper in a big red binder, with plenty of crossing out. She dreamt of romance herself, and after knowing her husband-to-be for only three weeks shocked her parents by accepting his marriage proposal and heading off to Surrey to live with him. Once there, she began writing romance again and discovered the wonderful world of Mills & Boon® Medical Romance™.

After four children—including a set of twins—and fifteen years of trying to get published, she finally received 'The Call'! Now she lives on Hayling Island, and when she's not busy as a First Responder she creates her stories wandering along the wonderful Hampshire coastline with her two dogs, muttering to herself and scaring the locals.

Visit Louisa on Twitter, @louisaheaton, on Facebook, www.facebook.com/Louisaheatonauthor, and on her website: www.louisaheaton.com

THE BABY THAT CHANGED HER LIFE
is Louisa Heaton's debut title
for Mills & Boon® Medical Romance™!

For Nicholas, James, Rebecca, Jared and Jack xxx

PROLOGUE

CALLIE TAYLOR STARED at the pregnancy test kit. She felt the weight of it in her hands. There was no point in reading the instructions—she already knew what they said. Knew the simplicity of its words: *'One line indicates a negative result. Two pink lines indicate a positive result'.*

Simple words but such a momentous implication. Life-changing. Well, just for nine months, maybe—because, as a surrogate, she'd be giving the baby away after it was born. But even then...being best friends with the father of the baby meant the baby would *always* be in her life...

Callie opened the box, pulling out the thick wad of paper wrapped around the end of the two kits, and threw the instructions in the bin. She knew how these things worked. As a midwife, she conducted many a test—especially when she worked in the fertility clinic. She placed the second kit back on the shelf and tore through the wrapping around the first.

She had never considered for even one moment that she would be doing this test on herself, and yet here she stood.

What was she doing? Had she made the right decision to do this? To be a surrogate? What if things didn't work out? What if she fell in love with the baby?

No, course not...I'd never do that.

She splashed her face with cold water and dried her hands.

Pee on the stick. That was all she had to do and she would *know*.

Could there be any doubt? It had to be positive, didn't it? She already felt sick and tired all the time. And she kept eating biscuits.

Not much of a sacrifice, though, was it? A big waistline and labour. That was all she had to get through to give Lucas and Maggie their much wanted baby. Callie could do that. And she didn't have to worry about wanting to keep the baby because she'd never wanted kids anyway.

No biggie.

So why aren't I peeing on this stick?

She held the slim white plastic tube in her fingers, staring at it. Her bladder felt full. There was only one thing to do…

She did what she had to and put the cap on the stick, sliding it between the taps on her sink.

I'll look at it in a moment.

Just as she was finishing washing her hands her doorbell rang. They were insistent, whoever they were. Ringing constantly, a finger held on the button, determined not to stop until she answered the door.

'Oh, God… Who is it?' she called out. If it was someone she didn't know, then she wasn't going to bother answering it at all! Did they not know that she had a life-changing moment going on here?

Leaving the bathroom, she glanced around at the state of her flat. It wasn't too bad. There were cups here and there and on the coffee table, papers, magazines and an open packet of gingernuts. Clothes were draped over the back of the sofa, the radiator, and the whole place had a bit of an uncared-for air about it. It looked a mess.

Like me. Besides I'm in my pyjamas.

'Callie, it's me...Lucas!'

Lucas. The father. Maybe...

Okay, I have to answer the door for you, at least.

'Hang on.' Callie moved quickly down her hallway, grabbing stray items of clothes and tossing them all in her bedroom. She ran her fingers through her hair, hoping she didn't look too much like death warmed up, and pulled open the door, trying to seem casual.

'Hi,' Lucas said. He looked awful.

She frowned. Lucas looked pale, distracted. Not his usual self.

Callie followed him into her lounge. 'You okay?'

It wasn't like Lucas just to turn up like this. Normally he'd ring to let her know he was coming round, just to make sure it was all right and she wasn't going out.

Lucas stood in the centre of Callie's lounge, hands in his jacket pockets, looking very uncomfortable. 'No, not really—no.' He fidgeted in his pockets, bit his lip. Then, with nothing better to do, he sat down on the couch in a sudden movement, waiting for Callie to join him.

'What's up?' She hoped this was going to be a quick conversation, considering the state her stomach was in.

Lucas shrugged, unable to meet her gaze. 'Everything. Everything's up.'

Callie felt awkward. Normally in this situation a friend would reach out, lay a reassuring hand on a knee and say, *Hey, what's up? You can tell me.* But Callie didn't feel comfortable doing that. It wasn't who she was. She didn't do reassuring physical contact.

Except with her patients. Somehow it seemed okay to do it with them. It was her professional persona. It wasn't *her.* That was *Midwife* Callie, not *Real* Callie.

Lucas smiled at her, but it was strained—one of those brave smiles that people tried to put on their faces when in reality the last thing they wanted to do was smile.

Callie was even more at a loss.

'Hey…what's wrong?' She edged closer. She could manage that and resist the urge to put her arm around him.

'It's Maggie…'

'What's wrong?' she asked quickly. 'Is she sick?' Callie really couldn't imagine anything worse than that.

'No, not sick. That would be easy to deal with… No, she's worse than sick.' His voice had a tinge of anger to it now, and Callie found herself frowning.

'Then what is it?' She dreaded asking. What would he say? Had she been in an accident? Was she at death's door? In a coma? If it were any of these things, then how would the baby situation work? She'd only agreed to be a surrogate because there was no chance she'd be expected to take care of the baby…

Oh, God, I'm going to be expected to take care of the baby…

Horror and fear grabbed her in their vice and she began to feel icy-cold, almost to the point of shivering. She closed her eyes at the onslaught, hoping that when she opened them again everything would be good and Lucas would tell her something nice.

Lucas took in a deep breath. 'She left. Walked out.'

He looked at her in disbelief and waited for her reaction. His eyes were strangely empty of tears, despite the news.

'*Left*? But—'

'She's been having an affair, apparently. Some doctor in A&E. I don't know—I think that's what she said. She said I didn't love her enough, she wasn't happy, and she's gone.' He stood up then, unable to sit still a second longer, sighing heavily now that he'd told her the important news. He turned to her and did that brave smile thing again. 'Good thing you're not pregnant yet.'

His words echoed around her skull like a bully taunting her in the playground.

Of course. She'd told neither Lucas nor Maggie about feeling a bit dodgy these last few days. She'd kept it to herself so that if it *were* true that she was having a baby it would be the best surprise to give them…

Only now it was backfiring as a great idea. There was a test in the bathroom, currently marinating, about to tell them both their future. She *could* be pregnant. With Lucas's child and no Maggie to play the part of mother!

So who would be mum, then?

Callie recoiled at the thought, looking away from Lucas and shifting back in her chair. She nibbled on her nail, worrying about all the implications.

She'd never wanted to be a mother—that was the whole point! It was her gift to Lucas and Maggie: the most perfect gift you could ever give to your best friend. A baby. Ten tiny fingers and ten tiny toes…all for them to look after, allowing her to swoop in occasionally on visits and bestow a few 'oohs' and 'aahs' before sweeping out again. The perfect—and distant—godparent.

And that was all. Callie wasn't meant to have a bigger role than that!

Sitting there, she felt numb. She knew she needed to go to the bathroom. To check that result. All she had to do was excuse herself…

Callie leapt to her feet and turned to Lucas to say something, but he'd gone. Her eyes tracked a movement to her left and she saw him disappearing into her bathroom…

'No!'

The bathroom door closed and she heard him lock the door.

Oh, God…

She waited.

And waited.

She heard the flush of her cistern, then the running of her sink taps. Closing her eyes in disbelief, she could see in her mind's eye him picking up the test on the sink and finding out that…

That what? It could still be negative, couldn't it? There was every possibility that the egg salad she'd eaten last night had been off. And the day before that? Maybe that jacket potato had been past its sell-by date…

Lucas emerged from the bathroom. He held the test in his hand and came back into her lounge, looking perplexed. His every step was heavy. Then his gaze met hers. 'You're pregnant?'

She stared at him, hearing the words but needing confirmation still. 'It's positive? Two lines?'

He turned it round so she could see and, yes, there were two solid pink lines.

Callie's mouth went dry. Sinking back down onto the couch, she felt her head sink into her hands. Tears burned her eyes with a fire she'd never felt before.

'You're pregnant.'

This time it wasn't a question.

Callie sat numb, aware only of Lucas sinking onto the couch next to her, just an inch or so away.

She hoped he wouldn't put his arm around her, or tell her everything was going to be okay, because how could he? How could he know?

Neither of them had any idea.

So they sat in silence, staring only at the carpet.

CHAPTER ONE

DR LUCAS GOLD sat next to Callie in the ultrasound waiting room, wishing he had something he could do with his hands. Nerves were running him through with adrenaline, and he had to fight the strong urge to get out of his seat and pace the floor.

He wasn't used to feeling out of his depth in the hospital. It was his home turf—the place he felt most secure. He knew what he was doing with work and he was looked up to and respected for it. But this situation was brand-new. Something he'd never experienced before. It was completely terrifying and he had no idea how to handle it. His insides were a mish-mash of conflicting thoughts and emotions, all jarring with each other and fighting for superiority, whilst on the outside he hoped he was maintaining an air of calm authority. As everyone was used to.

His best friend, Callie, was drinking water from a white plastic cup, an oasis of calm, whilst he sat there, rigid, a million thoughts running through his head.

'Callie Taylor?' A nurse in blue scrubs stood in a doorway.

He glanced at Callie, meeting her gaze and offering a supporting smile, although he knew he was probably just as nervous as she was. This situation was all just so... complicated! Not the way he'd imagined this time in his life being at all. But he tried not to show it. He didn't want Callie worrying. He didn't want her to think that he had any doubts at all.

Not that I do. Have doubts, that is. Not about the baby anyway.

And he knew that *she* just had to be as frightened of this as he was. The situation wasn't perfect, was it? For either of them. People didn't normally plan to have babies like this. But it was the situation they were in and he was going to make it work—no matter what. The important thing here was the baby, and he was determined to do right by his child as well as his best friend. After all, he was the one who'd got her into this mess. There were so many men who got a woman pregnant and then, when the circumstances changed, left them holding the baby.

Well, not me. I could never be that man.

They both stood and he reached out to touch her upper arm, just to offer her some reassurance. But something held him back and he stopped, letting his hand drop away, pretending not to have done it and hoping she hadn't noticed. She wasn't his to touch, after all.

'After you.'

He followed her into the darkened room and stood by her side. He held his hands out as she got onto the bed, to make sure she wasn't about to fall whilst she carried his precious cargo, before sitting down in the chair beside it.

The sonographer smiled at them both. 'Oh, Callie, I didn't realise it was you!' It was one of her colleagues: Sophie. 'Are you happy for me to perform your scan today?'

Callie nodded. ''Course!'

Sophie beamed. 'So exciting! Okay, can you confirm your name and date of birth for me?'

Callie gave the details.

'And it says here that this is your first pregnancy?'

'That's right.'

Callie's voice held a tremor and Lucas glanced at her, wondering what she was thinking.

'And when was the date of your last period?'

'February seventh.'

Sophie fiddled with the plastic wheel that Lucas knew was a predictor of delivery dates. 'So that makes you twelve weeks and two days today—is that right?'

'Yes.'

'Okay, so what I'm going to do is ask you to lower the waistband on your trousers. I'll put some gel on you, which might feel cold but will help the transducer move around easier and also helps with a better image. Now, do you have a full bladder?'

'Fit to burst.'

Sophie laughed. 'I'll try not to press on it too hard. So, do you want to just undo your trousers for me and lower the waist?'

Lucas glanced away, looking elsewhere to give Callie some privacy. He waited for Sophie to tuck some blue paper towel into the top of Callie's underwear before turning back. He watched the sonographer squirt on the gel, mentally hurrying her in his mind, but smiling when Callie gasped at the feel of it on her warm skin. Then he waited.

Sophie had the screen turned away from them both as she made her initial sweeps with the scanner, and Lucas had to fight every instinct in his body not to get up and go round the bed to have a look at the screen himself!

It was difficult to be the patient. To be the person on the other side. He was used to being the one who knew what was going on first. But he knew he had to wait. Sophie would be checking for an actual embryo first, then a heartbeat, before she turned the screen for them to see.

He'd have to learn how to be patient if he was going to be a good parent.

He glanced at Callie and noticed the frown on her face

in the half-light. He wanted to tell her it would be all right, to hold her hand tight in his and tell her that there was nothing for her to worry about, but he knew he couldn't. Not yet. What was the right etiquette in this situation? No one told you *that* at the clinic.

She's pregnant with my child and I daren't even touch her.

Besides, how could he tell her there was nothing to worry about? It wasn't true, was it? There was plenty to worry about. Like how this was going to work in the first place. Maggie was supposed to be by his side at this moment, both of them watching the screen with Callie, but Maggie was gone. That was still a shock. They were on their own now and he had no idea what Callie was thinking.

Then Sophie was smiling and turning the screen. 'There you are...your baby.'

'Oh, my God!'

Lucas couldn't quite believe it! After all the uncertainty—all the testing, the waiting, the drugs, the injections, the tests. After all this time... There it was. A tiny grey bean shape, nestling in Callie's womb, its tiny heart busily beating away. It was amazing. Surreal.

My child...

His eyes burned into the screen, imprinting the shape of his child, the beat of its strong heart, into his memory for ever. This was something that could never be forgotten. Pride filled his soul and he felt an instant connection and a surge of protectiveness for his little bean—and for Callie.

He'd waited so long for this moment...

To be a father...it's real...it's happening...

A laugh of relief escaped him and he reached out without thinking and grabbed Callie's hands in his, not noticing her flinch, forgetting that she wasn't good with physical contact. His prior fears were forgotten in the moment of joy.

'Can you believe it, Callie?'

She shook her head, not speaking, and he saw the welling of tears in her own eyes and was glad. He wouldn't normally be glad to see *anyone* well up with tears or cry, but this was different. They were in a difficult situation, the pair of them, thrown together into having a baby when they weren't even a couple. Now Maggie had gone they had to find a way through this situation themselves...

After Maggie had left them both in the lurch they'd initially struggled even to be in the same room as each other. It had been so hard to know what to do or say in their situation. And so wrong that they had to feel that way! They were best friends and always had been.

Maggie had been quick to see a solicitor and apply for a divorce. She'd said it was best for both of them. She'd been quick to sever all ties.

As the days had passed the atmosphere between him and Callie had got a little less awkward—though it still wasn't what it once had been. He knew Callie had as much adjustment to make to this situation as he had—if not more. It was a tough test of their friendship...one that neither of them could ever have imagined they would have to face. They were both testing the water like anxious ducklings, not knowing if they were going to sink or swim.

Each day that they worked together brought new challenges for both of them. He could sense her awkwardness each time she worked with him. Often he found himself craving the relaxed atmosphere they'd used to have with each other. The ability to laugh at the same things, to predict what the other was thinking.

Only last week he'd helped her out on a particularly difficult shoulder dystocia and, though they'd worked together efficiently for their patient, the old rapport had not been the same and he'd felt the tension between them return the second the baby had been delivered safely. When he'd left the patient's room he'd banged his fist against the wall with frustration at the whole situation.

But he was thrilled that seeing the baby meant something to Callie too. After all, he knew she'd never wanted to have a baby of her own. Not after the way she'd been treated by her own mother. Callie's childhood had been bloody awful compared to his. To see that she was just as affected as he was at seeing the baby onscreen was priceless.

'It's a baby,' she said.

Sophie laughed at them both. 'Of course it is!' She began to take measurements. She measured the head-to-rump length and then zoomed in on the nuchal fold, which was one of the measurements they took at the three-month scan to check the risk factors for Down syndrome. 'This all looks fine. Well within parameters.'

'That's good,' Lucas said, relieved.

'I had no idea you two were together. You kept that quiet,' Sophie said.

Callie glanced at him, a question in her eyes. Should they correct her?

'Actually…er…we're not…' He stumbled over the explanation, his words fading away as he recalled Maggie's impression of their relationship. '*You love Callie, Lucas! Always have! I could never live up to her, so now I'm giving you the chance to be together!*'

'We're not together,' Callie said. 'Just having a baby.'

Lucas gave a polite smile.

Sophie raised her eyebrows. 'There's no "just" about it—you two should know that. Having a baby is hard work.'

'You give all your patients this pep talk?' Lucas didn't want her attacking their decision, and he *certainly* didn't want Callie getting upset. She'd been through enough already, what with all the morning sickness and everything.

'I'm sorry. I didn't mean—'

Lucas shook his head, appalled that he'd been snappy

with her. 'I'm sorry. I didn't mean to be sharp with you/ It's just been a tough few months already.' What was he doing? He wasn't normally this prickly.

But Sophie was obviously used to the up-down moods of her patients and she smiled. 'That's all right. Here— take these.' She passed over a long strip of black-and-white scan photos.

Callie took the opportunity to pull free of his cradling hand and took the pictures first. She held them out before her, admiring each one, and then turned them so that Lucas could see. 'Look, Lucas.'

His heart expanded as he looked at each one. He could physically feel his love growing for this little bean-shaped creature he didn't yet know, but had helped create. All right, maybe not in the most ideal of circumstances, but they'd find a way to make it work. They had to. Even though he knew he and Callie would never be together *like that*.

'You okay?' He looked into her eyes and saw the tears had run down her cheeks now. He hoped they were happy tears. She *seemed* happy, considering...

'I'm good,' she said, nodding. 'You'd better take these.' She offered the pictures to him, but he sat back, shaking his head.

'Not all of them. I'll take half. You'll need some too.'

She looked puzzled, and he didn't like the look on her face. It made him feel uncomfortable to think that maybe she still didn't feel that the baby was part hers.

'It's your baby, too,' he insisted.

The smile left her face and Callie avoided his gaze, looking down and then wiping the gel from her belly using the paper towel.

He helped her sit up and turned away so she could stand and fasten her trousers. Then, when he judged enough time had passed, he turned back and smiled at her. 'Ready for work?'

'As I'll ever be.'

He thanked Sophie for her time and followed Callie, blinking in the brightness of the waiting room. He tried to avoid looking at all the couples holding hands. Couples in love, having a baby. The way *he* ought to be having a child with a partner.

Yet look at how I'm doing it.

He didn't want to think about how appalled his parents must be. He'd avoided talking to them about it, knowing they'd be sad that his marriage had failed. He was upset to have let them down, having wanted his marriage to succeed for a long time—like theirs had.

'Youngsters these days just give up on a relationship at the first sign of trouble!' his mother was fond of saying.

But I'd not given up. I thought everything was fine... We were going ahead with the surrogacy. It all looked good as far as I was concerned. And then...Maggie said it was over. That she'd found true love elsewhere because she'd had to!

Now he and Callie, his best friend in the whole wide world, were in this awkward situation.

We have to make this work.

I have to.

Callie had not expected to have such a strong emotional reaction to seeing the baby on screen. Why *would* she have suspected it? Having a baby had never been one of her dreams, had it? Not really. She'd always been happy to let other people have the babies. She just helped them along in their journey from being a woman to a mother. Others could have the babies—others could make the mistakes. Others could be utter let-downs to their children and be hated by them in the long run. Because that was what happened. In real life.

What did people say about not being able to choose your family?

So even though she'd *known* she was pregnant, logically, had *known* she was carrying a child, she'd still somehow been knocked sideways by seeing it on screen. Her hypothetical surrogate pregnancy had turned into a real-life, bona fide baby that she might have to look after! And seeing it on screen had made her feel so guilty and so upset, because she already felt inadequate. She feared that this baby would be born into a world where its mother was useless and wouldn't have a clue. Callie could already imagine its pain and upset.

Because she knew what it was like to have a mother like that.

Callie waited until the sonographer had led someone else into the scanning room and then she stopped Lucas abruptly. 'Hold this,' she said, passing him her handbag. 'I need to use the loo.' Her bladder was *killing* her! Sophie had pressed down hard, no matter what she'd said about being gentle.

In the bathroom, she washed her hands and then realised how thirsty she was and that she wanted a coffee. Her watch said that they had twenty minutes before they were due to start their shift, so when she went back outside she tried to ignore the anxious look on Lucas's face and suggested they head to the café.

'You okay with coffee?' Lucas asked with concern.

'I think so.' She'd been off coffee for weeks. But now she could feel an intense craving for one and ordered a latte from the assistant. 'This is so strange,' she said as she gathered little sachets of sugar and a wooden stirrer.

Lucas looked about them, glancing at the café interior. 'What is?'

'This.'

'Having coffee?' He smiled.

She gave him a look. 'You know what I mean! This. The *situation*. Me and you—having a baby. I mean…' She swallowed hard, then asked him the question that had been on her mind ever since Maggie had walked away. The question that had been keeping her awake at night. The question that she wasn't even sure she wanted answered. If he said he wanted her to be the mother… 'How's it going to work?'

She could tell her question had him stumped.

He was trying to decide how to answer her. After all, it wasn't an easy situation. After Maggie's big revelation they'd both been knocked for six—especially when Maggie had kept her word and disappeared out of their lives altogether. No one had heard a peep from her—not even the hospital where she'd worked. She'd really dropped them in it as they'd lost a midwife without notice!

For a while Callie had believed that at some point Maggie would call and it would all sort itself out again. That she and Lucas had simply had one giant misunderstanding and it would all be sorted easily. Because then it would be easier for *her*. *Callie*. And wasn't that how Lucas operated? Before Maggie there'd been other girlfriends. There'd certainly been no shortage of them during the time she'd known him. Which seemed like forever. He'd always been splitting up with them and then getting back together again.

But Maggie hadn't called. The situation hadn't changed.

Callie was pregnant with Lucas's child. But they hadn't slept together and they weren't a couple.

Lucas wanted a baby and Callie never had.

Yet here she was. Pregnant. And though she'd thought she'd be safe getting pregnant, because she wouldn't be in any danger of having to keep the baby, she was now in the predicament that she might have to. Or at least have more to do with it than she'd hoped.

It.

'Honestly, Callie…? I don't know how it's going to work. But I know that it *will*. In time. We'll sort something out.'

He stood opposite her and shook some sugar into his own drink, replaced the lid.

'But *how* do you know that?' She pressed him for more information. He was her best friend in the whole wide world and always had been—for as long as she could remember. There'd once been a moment—a brief, ever so tempting moment—when she'd considered what it would be like to go out with him, but she'd not allowed herself to do it. His friendship with her had been much too valuable and the one stable element in her wretched childhood.

Callie didn't do relationships. Not long-term ones anyway. She'd had dates, and gone out with someone for a couple of months, but once he'd started making mutterings about commitment she'd backed off.

Then one day Lucas had asked her out. On a date. In a boyfriend/girlfriend kind of way. He'd looked so nervous when he'd asked her. And though they'd been great friends, and she'd known she loved him a lot, she just hadn't been about to ruin their friendship by going out on a date with him.

Lucas had been her one stable choice through her childhood and she couldn't risk losing him if things went wrong between them. Besides, they'd both been about to go off to university—it would never have worked, would it? It had been a sensible decision to make.

She could still recall the absolute shock on his face when she'd turned him down. But then he'd left her that night and gone out and met Maggie and the whole thing had been moot, after all.

'I don't know it. But you're sensible—so am I. We're good friends. *Best* friends. I don't see why we won't be able to come to some arrangement.'

She watched him sip and then wince at his coffee. 'I wish I could be as sure as you,' she said. Because Callie wasn't used to certainties. All her life she'd felt as if she lived in limbo—nothing stable, nothing rooted, her mother going through bottles of alcohol as fast as she went through various men, all of them the latest, greatest love of Maria's life.

He put his coffee down and reached out to take her hand, knowing she didn't feel comfortable with personal touch but doing it anyway to make his point. His thumb stroked the back of her knuckles, gently caressing the skin. 'We'll be fine.'

Then he let go and went back to his coffee.

She was relieved he'd let go—relieved to get back control of her hand. Relieved the sizzling reaction to his touch—where had *that* come from?—had gone. Her hand had lit up with excited nerves as his fingers had wrapped around hers and her stomach had tumbled all over like an acrobat when he'd squeezed them tight before letting go.

She gave a little laugh to break the tension. 'Too big a subject when we're due to start work in ten minutes!' She grinned, but inside her mind was racing. She'd never reacted like that to Lucas before. Why? What was happening? Hormones? Possibly…

No, it *had* to be. No 'possibly' about it.

He smiled back, laughing too. 'Way too big.'

Callie laughed nervously. There'd been something reassuring and caring about his touch, and though she disliked physical contact something had changed since she'd got pregnant. It was as if she needed it now but didn't know how to ask for it, having gone for so long without it.

And how threatening was Lucas's touch anyhow? He was her best friend. It didn't mean anything. Not like *that*. And he knew it.

But I'd like you to protect me, Lucas. Promise me I'll be safe.

Lucas sat in his office, twiddling with a pen without really seeing it. There was plenty of work he knew he ought to be getting on with, but his mind was caught up in a whirl of thoughts and emotions. As it had been for many weeks now.

Maggie was gone. But if he was honest with himself that wasn't what was bothering him. Not at all. What bothered him was what Maggie had said on that final night before she'd walked out.

'I tried with you, Lucas, I really tried! But it was all pointless, wasn't it? You've never truly loved me. Not the way you should have.'

'Of course I love you—'

She'd half laughed, half cried.

'But it wasn't real, Lucas! You thought it was, and that was the problem. You lost your heart to Callie long ago and you can't see it!'

'Callie? No, you're wrong. She's my friend...that's all—'

'She's more than your friend and I can't be second best in your life. I need someone to love me for me. I don't want to be your substitute.'

'You're not! Maggie, you're being ridiculous. Callie and I are just friends and that's all we'll ever be!'

'But you still want more. Haven't you noticed how un-comfortable it is for me every time she comes round? How you are with her?'

He'd looked at her then, confused and still reeling from her announcement that she was leaving him.

'Well, yes, but—'

'I know you care for me, Lucas. Maybe you do love me—just not enough. And not in the way that you should.'

'But we're going to have a baby together, Maggie. Hope-fully. One day soon!'

She'd looked at him then, her eyes filled with sadness.

'And look who you picked to carry your child.'

Why had he allowed Callie to get into his mess? His beautiful Callie. His best friend. That was all she was. He knew her situation, knew her background—with her awful childhood and her ridiculous drunk of a mother—and he'd stupidly let her get into this situation.

Why?

Was it because Callie always seemed to set things right? Was it because he only had happy memories with her, so he'd let her suggest the surrogacy in the hope that her involvement would somehow set his marriage right?

Maybe. He couldn't be sure.

But now his mess had got real. There was a *baby*. He'd just seen it. And though he was happy, and thrilled to be having a child—there was no disappointment in *that*—he wasn't sure how all of this was going to sort itself out.

He didn't want to pretend. As he had with Maggie. The fact that he'd hurt Maggie hurt him. Pretend to Callie that everything would be fine…? He couldn't be sure. Not really. Callie didn't think she could be a mother so it looked as if he was going to have to raise this baby by himself.

I could do that. Plenty of men are single dads.

But the realisation was there that he *did* want Callie involved. More than she had ever volunteered for.

Was that fair of him? To push her down a road she wasn't ready for? Did he want to parent a baby with someone who wasn't committed—like his father?

The pen dropped to the table with a clatter and he glanced at the clock. He needed to be with his patients.

I'll have to think about this later.

He and Callie could do this. He was sure of it.

Callie was running the booking clinic that afternoon, and there were twelve women booked in to be seen over the next four hours. Due to Maggie's unexpected absence they were still down a staff member and had had to rely on an agency midwife to step into the breach and help out.

Callie took a few minutes to show the new member of staff where everything was, and how to log into the computer system, and then pulled out the first file: *Rhea Cart-wright. Sixteen years old.*

Callie checked to make sure she had all the equipment she'd need and then went to the waiting room and called out the girl's name. A young girl, who was there alone and looked far less than sixteen, stood up. Clasping a large bag in front of her stomach, she followed Callie into the clinic room.

'Hi, there. My name's Callie Taylor. I'm a midwife here at St Anne's and I'll be following your case throughout your pregnancy—hopefully right up to the birth. How are you feeling today?'

The girl was about eleven weeks pregnant, according to the notes from her GP, so Callie hoped she was no longer suffering the effects of morning sickness as she herself had done. Those few weeks when it had been at its worst had been just horrible!

'I'm all right.'

The girl answered tersely, without smiling, and didn't meet Callie's eye as she gazed about the room, taking in the breastfeeding poster, the framed black-and-white picture of a baby fast asleep surrounded by sunflowers in full colour.

Callie beckoned her to sit down and settled into a chair next to her. 'No one with you today?'

'My mum couldn't make it. She was busy.'

She nodded. Perhaps Rhea's mum *was* busy. Or perhaps Rhea's mum had no idea of the pregnancy—or, worse still, couldn't be bothered. Callie didn't *want* to jump to that conclusion, but she had personal experience of having an uninterested mother. It wasn't nice. But she couldn't judge someone she'd never met, and nor did she want to jump to conclusions.

'What about your partner? The baby's father?'

Rhea shook her head and looked at anything but Callie. 'I don't want to talk about him.'

She was going to be a closed book. Callie knew she would have to tread softly with Rhea and gain the girl's confidence if she was to learn anything. It was like this sometimes with teenage mothers. They suddenly found themselves in an adult world, living by adult rules, when all they wanted was to live by their own and be left to get on with it.

And in Callie's experience pregnant teenage mothers were often reluctant to show their trust until you'd earned it.

'Okay…well, take a seat.' Rhea still hadn't sat down. 'I'll need to run through some questions with you.'

She tried to keep her voice gentle and neutral. Nothing forceful. Nothing that would suggest Rhea was being ordered or expected to answer questions, as if she was taking some sort of test.

'Just some basic things about you and your last period… that sort of thing. Is that okay?'

Rhea sank into the chair with her bag clasped in front of her, still looking at anything but Callie. She shrugged, as if unwilling to commit either way.

'Well, we'll just start with some basics and see how we go on. Can you confirm your date of birth for me?'

Callie sensed it was going to be a long afternoon. Rhea was not going to give up any information easily. Small red flags were waving madly in her mind. Her midwife's sixth sense, developed over time, was telling her that there was something going on here that she didn't know about. She had learned that it was best to listen to it. It would be so straightforward if every couple or single mother she saw had a happy home life for a baby to be born into, but quite often that wasn't the case. There was a lot of poverty in London. There were a lot of drugs problems, lots of drink problems. Hadn't that been her own experience?

'April the first.'

April Fools' Day. Not a joke. It was confirmed in her

notes. Callie knew she didn't have the type of relationship with Rhea yet to make a joke about the date, so she kept a neutral face and voice and continued with her questions.

'And when was the first day of your last menstrual period?'

There was a moment of silence, as if Rhea was weighing up whether to give her the information or not, then she said, 'February the seventh.'

The same as me.

Callie smiled, about to say so, but decided to hold back. This young girl was so different from her in so many ways.

'Do you mind telling me whether this is a planned pregnancy, or were you using contraception?' she asked without thinking.

She'd not asked just because Rhea was a teenager. It was one of the questions that she always asked. It was important to know whether someone had planned their pregnancy. Whether they'd been actively trying for a baby, or whether the pregnancy was a complete accident and a surprise. It had a bearing on the mother's attitude to it all. Just because a mother was at her booking visit it didn't automatically mean that she wanted to keep the baby. Plus, she needed to know if Rhea had taken any prenatal vitamins.

'I don't see why that's important.'

Callie put down her pen. 'I'm sorry. I just wanted to know whether you'd planned the pregnancy or not.'

'Because I'm sixteen? Because I'm young it must have been a mistake? Is that what you're saying?'

Rhea met Callie's gaze for the first time, and now Callie could see how frightened and unsure this young girl was.

Where was her support? She was so *young*! It had to be scary for her. Callie herself was twenty-eight—a whole twelve years older than Rhea—and *she* was terrified of being pregnant. How could she even begin to imagine how this girl felt?

'No, not at all. I didn't mean that. It's a standard question—'

'Well, I don't want to talk about it. Next?'

Rhea folded her arms and closed up and didn't meet Callie's eyes again for the rest of the meeting.

It was obvious she was a troubled young woman, and if Callie was going to be there for her then she needed to get the young girl on side.

'Let's start again... Let's look at your family health. Any medical problems on your side of the family I should know about? Diabetes? Asthma?'

Rhea shook her head reluctantly. 'We're fine.'

'Again this is a standard question: any history of depression? Anything like that?'

'My mum has that.'

Right, okay—that's something.

'Do you know if your mum suffered with postnatal depression?'

'No.'

'That's okay.' Voice still neutral. Unthreatening. Soft. Rhea was answering the questions.

'What about the father of the baby?'

Rhea stiffened, still not meeting her gaze, shuffling her feet, twiddling with her bag strap with nervous fingers. 'What about him?'

'Any health issues on his side we should be concerned about?'

'I don't know.'

What is it about the father of this baby that she doesn't want me to know?

'How tall is he?'

'What?' Rhea frowned.

'His height? It can have a bearing on the size of your baby.'

Surely she can tell me his height?

'I don't know.'

Callie paused. What was going on here? How did she not know the boy's height? Or perhaps she did know but didn't want to give Callie any clues that might identify him? Perhaps he was an older man? Married? Or was he younger than Rhea? Which would be a whole different kettle of fish. Not that she wanted to think that way, but it was a possibility she had to consider.

'How did you two meet?' That *wasn't* a standard question, but Callie felt she needed to do some extra detective work on this case if she were to get any helpful answers.

'What's that got to do with anything?'

Callie shrugged. 'I'm just interested.'

'Nosy, more like. How I got pregnant has got nothing to do with you. You're a midwife. You should know how people get pregnant, yeah? So just tell me what I need to do next so I can get out of here.'

Callie shrank back from the anger, but she was getting really concerned for Rhea. The girl was so angry and scared. There had to be a way to help her. To get the young girl to trust her.

'Okay, okay... I guess what I really need to know is your intention. You're very young and I have no idea of your support system. I'm making no judgements, but I need to know what your intentions are regarding this pregnancy.'

'My intentions?'

'Yes. Are you keeping it? Are you here to ask about other options?' She didn't want to use the word abortion unless Rhea used it first.

She was quiet for a while, and Callie could see that Rhea's eyes were filling with tears. Her nose was going red and she was really fighting the urge to cry. All Callie's instincts told her to reach out and comfort her, to put an arm around her, to show her that someone genuinely cared. But it wouldn't have been professional to break that boundary—

and, besides, she wasn't comfortable being that person just yet with Rhea. Any show of affection might have the opposite effect and send Rhea running for the hills.

So she sat quietly and waited, her gaze on Rhea's face.

'I don't want it.' Her voice was quiet and empty of emotion.

'You don't?' This was what she'd suspected.

'No.'

'Then there are two options open to you, Rhea.'

Tears rolled down Rhea's cheeks. 'I can't have an abortion. I don't believe in it.'

'Right…okay.'

'I want to give it away. Get rid of it that way.'

It.

So impersonal. So unattached.

I called my baby 'it'.

There had to be personal reasons for Rhea's decision, but Callie truly felt that now was not the time to push for them. If Rhea wanted to give her baby away after it was born, that gave Callie six more months of learning about Rhea and working with her to find out what was going on and how best she could help her.

It was a big decision to give away your baby.

It was what I was going to do. Give the baby to Lucas and Maggie. Only it's not 'the' baby now. It's 'my' baby, isn't it?

Isn't it?

Callie wasn't sure. She and Lucas still hadn't discussed properly what they were going to do to sort this. But they needed to. They were on the clock now and time was ticking. Should she still give the baby to Lucas? Was it even her decision to make?

Callie decided that once the booking clinic was over she was going to call the fertility clinic and ask to speak to one of the counsellors there. She, Lucas and Maggie had each undertaken individual counselling before agreeing to the surrogacy, but the situation had changed now. Everything was different.

I was going to give my baby away. Happily. I was going to do it for Lucas and Maggie.

Who was Rhea doing it for? *What* was Rhea doing it for?

'Okay. We can talk about that. It's a big decision.'

'I know what I'm doing.'

'Have you talked to your family about it?'

'It's not their decision. It's mine. My body—my choice.'

'Of course it is. I'm not denying that.'

'Just put it in my notes that I'm giving it away. The Social can have it. I don't want to see it, or hold it. Just get them to take it away and give it to someone who doesn't know where it's come from.'

'Doesn't know where it's come from'? Why would she say that? Did Maria think that way about me? She never wanted me. Never wanted anything to do with me. Was my own mother like this young girl once?

'I'll put it in your notes. You do know that I'll be here for you throughout this, Rhea? Any time. You'll be able to call me, night or day. I'll give you my contact details.' She passed over a small card that had the hospital numbers and Callie's own personal mobile number on it too.

Rhea stuffed it into her bag. 'I don't want anyone judging me.'

'No one will do that.'

'You don't know what I've been through.'

'No. But I'm hoping that at some point you'll trust me enough to tell me.'

She meant it. Sincerely she meant it. And she hoped Rhea could sense that. It was at times like these that Callie's job meant the world to her. It was at times like these when she felt she could really help someone—and this young girl clearly needed help for something.

If only she'd let me in. If only she'd let me help her so that another baby doesn't grow up feeling like I did as a child. Unwanted and unloved.

'Don't you need to take my blood pressure or something?'

Rhea broke the silence and Callie nodded, glad that Rhea was offering her something.

'Of course. I need to take blood, too.'

'I brought this.' Rhea reached into her bag and took out a small jar with a urine sample in it. 'I washed it out before I used it.'

'That's great—thanks.' She would need another sample if this one was more than two hours old. It was hospital policy. However, she wasn't going to say that. Rhea had offered her a little something. That would have to do for now.

Rhea's blood pressure was fine, as was her urine sample. Nothing out of the ordinary and all well within parameters. Physically, she seemed fine. It was just emotionally that something was off.

'You know, I'm really looking forward to getting to know you better throughout this, Rhea.'

'Yeah, well, don't go thinking you'll get me to change my mind.'

'That's not my place.'

'No, it isn't. No one has the right to judge me for giving this thing away.'

'No, they haven't.' *I was going to give a baby away myself.* 'But please don't call the baby a "thing". Call it what it is.'

Rhea stood up to go and slung her bag over her shoulder. 'It's a *thing*. It will always be a *thing*. It'll never be anything else.' And she stormed from the clinic.

Callie watched her go, bewildered and amazed. In some ways Rhea seemed so strong, but in others she was just a tiny young girl, terrified and afraid.

And what am I afraid of?

Callie's hand went to her own stomach, as yet still un-changed in size. She didn't even know she was doing it until her phone beeped a text message alert and she was brought back into the present. As she rummaged in her bag for her phone thoughts echoed through her mind.

Don't go getting attached.

You have no idea if you're keeping it either.

CHAPTER TWO

THE NEXT DAY Callie was scheduled to work on a twin delivery. She could see that Lucas was on duty that day too, along with the senior consultant Dev Patel, though she hadn't seen him yet. They had four women in labour, most in early stages, and Callie had been assigned to a woman in her late forties, having her first babies. Callie hadn't been expecting to work with Lucas, but he was already in the room.

'There's been some decelerations,' he said, after saying hello and seeing her look of surprise.

Olivia Hogarth was on her knees, leaning over the back of the bed, panicking and almost out of control, showing real signs of not dealing with her labour at all. Every time a contraction came along a terrified look came into Olivia's eyes and she began to huff and puff on the Entonox as if for dear life. Her husband, James, stood helpless beside her. He was at a complete loss as to what to do, but kept rubbing her back for dear life as she held on to the support of the bed.

'Hi, Olivia, I'm Callie, and I'm going to be your midwife today.' Callie leant round the back of the bed so Olivia could see her face and not just hear a random voice.

'Hurgh!' Olivia's teeth gripped the mouthpiece and her frightened gaze practically begged Callie to do something. 'Help me!'

'Okay…slow, deep breaths…that's it. Slow your breathing.' Callie showed Olivia how to breathe in slowly through her nose for five seconds and then out through her mouth for five more seconds.

'I'm all tingly!' Olivia protested when the contraction was over. 'Pins and needles.'

'It's because you're not exhaling properly. Come on—practise with me whilst there's no contraction.'

As Olivia practised Callie took a moment to glance at Olivia's trace. There were some decelerations in the babies' heartbeats. Not by much, but they were definitely there. Each time Olivia's babies got squeezed by a contraction the heart-rate dipped, which meant they weren't liking labour very much.

Callie wasn't happy with the trace and glanced up at Lucas as he came to stand by her and judge it for himself.

Sometimes decelerations could be caused by there being a short cord, or a knot in the cord, or by the cord being tightly wrapped around the baby's body. It didn't mean that there was something wrong with the baby physically. But Callie knew it was never worth taking any chances. It was always best to call for help if you were working alone. If you weren't sure you got someone else. Fortunately she already had Lucas there.

He stood beside her, dressed all in black, in tailored shirt and trousers, and she could smell his aftershave. Since she'd got pregnant smells and aromas had seemed particularly pronounced, and his was delicious today.

Callie glanced at him sideways as he concentrated on the trace. Her heart skipped a beat—*palpitations?* She'd never had those before—it had to be the pregnancy. She supposed she couldn't help it, she thought wryly. He was a very attractive man after all. Hadn't she watched a multitude of women fawn over him?

He was tall, broad and handsome. It was hard to think

that the little boy she'd once known—the one with the spindly legs and constantly scuffed knees—had turned into this strong, mature, devastatingly handsome man. It never mattered what was going on in her own life—her mother letting her down yet again, her mother lying to her, someone treating her badly—she always brightened when she saw Lucas. He was her pillar. Her rock. Her safe place in stormy seas. He'd always been there for her and she hoped he always would be. Especially now. Now they were having a baby together—even if it wasn't in the traditional way.

He looked really good today. Fresher and brighter-looking than she'd seen him look these last few weeks. Maggie leaving the way she had, and admitting to an affair, had shaken them both. But even though Lucas had been shocked by the end of his marriage, he'd thankfully not been devastated. He'd coped with the change in his life amazingly well, and she couldn't help but admire him for his courage and resilience—as everyone did.

She could only assume that seeing the scan yesterday had perked him up. Either that or he'd managed a great night's sleep! His eyes were bright and blue, like cornflowers in a summer meadow, and there was colour to his cheeks. He'd even shaved! These last few weeks he'd been beginning to look like a mountain man.

She liked the fact that he looked bigger and stronger. It made her feel safe and protected, and she knew he'd move heaven and earth to do anything to help her at the moment.

Callie couldn't help but wonder what this pregnancy was *doing* to her? Her emotions and responses seemed hyper-aware, with all these hormones floating about, and she knew she needed to be careful that she didn't let them carry her away. He cared for her because they were good friends. Nothing more.

He's just my friend. Yes, he's the baby's father, but it's not like we slept together, is it? It was all done in a petri dish in a clinic—nothing romantic.

But just thinking about sleeping with Lucas made her cheeks flush with heat.

She knew she needed to focus on her patient and deliberately stepped away from him. Thoughts about sleeping with Lucas were dangerous and she'd never allow them to surface.

Olivia finished puffing on her gas and air and looked panicked, her eyes open wide. 'What's wrong? Is it the babies?'

Lucas pulled out the long white roll of paper and checked through the tracing with Callie. He gave a tiny nod. 'Olivia, Baby A seems to be a bit upset after each contraction and Baby B doesn't look too happy either. It may just be because of the reduced room in your uterus and the contractions, but I'd like to be on the safe side.' He turned to Callie. 'When was her last examination?'

She checked the notes. 'Four and a half hours ago. Would you like me to do another?' They tried to examine women vaginally every four hours during labour. This usually gave the cervix plenty of time to show the changes every midwife and mother wanted to feel.

Lucas turned the full beam of his attention on the mother. 'Sure. Olivia, we'd like to examine you, if possible, see how you're getting along. Is that all right?'

'Of course.'

Lucas looked at Callie and nodded.

'I'll be as gentle as I can…'

Callie washed her hands and then put on gloves, settling herself on the side of Olivia's bed as she did so. She felt as much as she could, her fingers sweeping the edge of the cervix, her eyes on Lucas.

He kept checking with Olivia to make sure she was all right and apologising for any discomfort she might be feeling, but Olivia was quite stoical. The most calm she'd been since Callie had met her. Perhaps she could cope better with men around, supporting her, rather than another woman?

As Callie removed her gloves she smiled. 'You're making good progress. Eight centimetres.'

'Eight!' Olivia began to suck in gas and air again as another contraction hit, so she didn't notice Callie take Lucas to one side of the room.

'I'm concerned there's some extra blood in the birth canal,' she whispered. 'I don't want to panic her, but I think we need to put a continuous CTG on her and the babies and keep it monitored.' CTG was cardiotocography—a technical way of recording the foetal heartbeats as well as any uterine contractions.

'Yes, we need to be alert for any signs of possible placental abruption.' He kept his voice low.

Placental abruption was a life-threatening condition in which the placenta detached itself from the uterine wall before birth, causing heavy bleeding and potentially fatal consequences for both mother and baby if not caught in time.

'Possibly.'

'Okay. I want to move her to Theatre, just in case.'

'I'll ring Theatre to let them know we're coming.'

And just as Callie said this blood soaked into the sheets around Olivia's legs.

Her husband, James, leapt to his feet. 'My God! What's going on?'

Callie and Lucas leapt into action. There wasn't much time. They had to act fast. They quickly unplugged Olivia from the monitors, grabbed the ends of the bed and began to wheel her from the room.

Lucas kept his voice calm, yet firm, as he gave an explanation to James and Olivia. 'Your wife's bleed may mean the placenta has detached early from the wall of her womb. We need to do an emergency Caesarean to get the babies out safely.' Lucas's controlled, assertive voice was an oasis of calm in a situation that could so easily be filled with panic or fear.

'Is she going to be okay?' The colour had gone from James's face.

Olivia looked pale and clammy and her head was beginning to loll back against the pillows.

'Just follow us. It's going to be a general anaesthetic, so you won't be allowed into Theatre, I'm afraid.'

They began to push the bed from the room and head up the corridors towards the operating rooms. Lucas called out to passing staff to help and they responded to his firm authority and helped them get Olivia to Theatre.

'And the babies?'

As they reached the theatre doors there was a large sign stating 'Staff Only Beyond This Point' and James slowed to a stop, looking lost and hopeless.

Lucas turned back briefly and laid a reassuring hand on James's arm. 'We'll do our best for all of them.' And then he and Callie pushed Olivia into Theatre, leaving James behind, bewildered and in shock.

They didn't like to do it, but James was not their first priority at this point. Time was critical now, and they couldn't waste it by stopping to talk it through with Olivia's husband. They could debrief him afterwards.

It was a mad rush of preparation. They'd not had time to call Theatre, so the first the theatre staff knew of an emergency coming was when they wheeled Olivia in. But they were such a well-oiled machine that they all knew what to do.

Within minutes, they had Olivia under general anaesthetic, drapes up, and Lucas was scrubbed and ready to go. The theatre staff were used to emergency sections, and they all liked working with Lucas, who was calm and fair and friendly—unlike some of the other doctors who operated.

Lucas could just give a look and everyone would know what he needed. His authority was not questioned, and everyone in his team looked to him for guidance.

'I'm going to perform a lower segment section.' He pointed the scalpel to Olivia's skin and in one quick yet sure movement began the emergency operation.

Callie stood by the side of the bed, her heart pounding, her legs like jelly. She really disliked occasions such as this. *Emergencies.* If she could have her way then all babies would be born normally, without danger, without the need for Theatre. Babies were meant to arrive in calm environments, with music softly playing in the background, and then to be placed in their mother's arms afterwards for that all-important cuddle and skin-to-skin contact.

General anaesthetics and emergencies took away all of that. Babies were separate from their mothers until the mother was awake enough to hold the baby without dropping it, and sometimes that initial important breastfeed was missed because the mother was unable to do it, or the baby itself was too drowsy from the cross-over of the drugs the mother had had.

Her lips felt dry beneath the paper mask. She glanced at Lucas, admiring the concentration in his gaze, his composure. Despite the emergency, he knew exactly what needed to be done and how. But as she stood there Callie realised she was beginning to feel a little bit woozy and hot.

The rush from Olivia's room and pushing the bed through the corridors wouldn't normally have taken its toll, but now that she was pregnant she felt a little more fragile than normal. She still felt out of breath from the sprint and her brow was becoming sweaty, as was her top lip. Her stomach began to churn like a washing machine, as if she was about to be sick.

It wasn't the sight of the blood. That sort of thing never bothered her. Nor was it the controlled tension in the room.

No. This was something else. She didn't feel right at all. She looked at Lucas over her mask in a panic, hoping he'd look up. See her. Notice that something was wrong.

She could feel something...a weird sensation beginning to overcome her. If she could try to focus on his calm, reassuring face she felt it might help, but her vision was going a bit blurry and the noises in the room—the beeping of machines—began to sound distant and echoing.

As she felt herself sway slightly she put one hand on the bed to steady herself. Lucas looked up from his work and frowned.

'Callie? You okay?'

But his words sounded as if they were coming from far away. She blinked to clear her eyesight, felt her heart pound like a hammer and then heard a weird whooshing noise in her ears. A black curtain descended and she went crashing to the floor, taking a tray of instruments down with her.

'Callie!'

Lucas was unable to catch her. She'd been standing on the other side of the operating table and there was a patient between them. Instead he had to stand there, horrified, his scalpel poised, as she collapsed onto the floor and lay there, despite the best efforts of the scrub nurse to try and catch her.

Her arms were outspread, her eyes closed.

I need to concentrate on my patient first. Her life is in my hands. I'll have to let the others take care of Callie.

The situation killed him, but what could he do? Just focus on delivering Olivia safely and *then* he could check on Callie.

How did I not see she looked pale? he berated himself inwardly.

The anaesthetist couldn't move either, but two other theatre assistants got Callie up onto a trolley and wheeled her from the theatre. He watched her go, his heart in his mouth, his mind whooshing with a million thoughts. But he pulled it back.

I need to be professional. Callie's in good hands. I know that. I can't do anything here but look after my patient.

The staff were great. They knew the situation—knew Callie was Lucas's surrogate, and knew how much it must be hurting him not to be with her—so they all did their best to help him work quickly, so he could be with her.

Lucas had to think fast and concentrate. All he wanted to do was leave Theatre and go and check on Callie, but he *knew* he couldn't! His professional integrity told him to stay with his patient. Her life and that of her babies were on the line.

Once into the uterus, he was able to deliver both babies quickly. They came out crying, which was great. A glance at the monitors assured him that Olivia was doing fine, despite the emergency.

A few moments later the theatre assistants returned.

'How's Callie?' he asked, busy removing the placentas.

'Coming round. We left her in the staffroom with one of the midwives looking after her,' the assistant called, her back to him as she assessed the babies at the Resuscitaires.

'How are the babies?'

'Pinking up—we'll get there,' confirmed the paediatrician, and then there was a lusty cry and Lucas was able to let out a breath he hadn't realised he'd been holding. He glanced at the anaesthetist at the head of his patient.

'Sats ninety-seven per cent, BP dropped. But she's stable…she's good.'

That was good to know. He'd expected Olivia's blood pressure to drop with the bleed, but if she was stable then it looked as if both mother and twins were going to get through this.

Once both the placentas were out Lucas began to stitch,

sewing together all the layers of muscle and fascia that made up the abdomen, finally closing Olivia's lower belly about forty-five minutes after he'd first had to open her.

It had been nearly thirty minutes since Callie's collapse and he was desperate to see her. His stomach was in knots, but he sewed quickly and efficiently. He kept clenching and unclenching his jaw as he thought of all the things that were worrying him.

Why did she faint? *Was* it a faint? Or something else? Perhaps she'd not eaten properly that morning? There had to be a reason, and he intended to do a full medical check-up on her when he got out of Theatre.

Why was everything going wrong? Having a child was meant to be one of the happiest times of his life! Yet it was all such a mess. He still didn't know what was going to happen after the birth, and now Callie had collapsed. He hated not being able to be there for her and he wanted to be. Every step of the way.

Finally Olivia was ready to go through to Recovery. The assistant and porters wheeled her away and he thanked the staff, seeing their appreciative smiles and nods, then scrubbed clean, quickly changed his scrubs and hurried off to find Callie.

He found her looking pale and ashen in the staffroom, feet up on the chairs and her hands shaking as she nursed a hot sweet tea.

He rushed straight over to her, kneeling by her side and feeling her forehead. 'Are you all right?'

She looked sheepish and slightly disturbed by his hand on her head, so he removed it.

'I'm fine.' Her voice sounded weak and shaky.

'You passed out.' He knew he sounded angry and was stating the obvious, but...

'I'm fine.'

'How do I know that?' Next he reached for her wrist and

felt her pulse as he glanced up at the clock in the room. Her skin was cool and soft, but her pulse was going quite fast. She pulled her hand free.

'Honestly, Lucas. I'm fine.' She sounded angry.

He knelt next to her, filled with concern, wanting to ask her a million questions, wanting to know if she'd hurt herself when she fell. He checked her over—skin pallor, pupil dilation, carotid pulse, respirations.

'You've no pain?'

'No. How's Olivia and the twins?'

'All doing well. Which is the least that can be said for you.'

'I missed breakfast, that's all.'

'That's *all*? You know how important breakfast is in your condition.'

'I know!'

'And yet you missed it? Why? What were you doing?' He tried his best not to sound angry, but knew she could hear it in his voice.

She shrugged, looking guilty. 'I slept in.'

'You *slept in*?'

'I was late getting up. I hit the snooze button a few times and then it was too late to eat breakfast, so I came straight to work. I was going to grab a banana or something.'

'So all you've had is that tea?'

'Yes.' She at least managed to look shamefaced.

He frowned, thinking of how he could immediately put this right. 'Wait there. Don't move.'

Lucas disappeared from the staffroom, headed for the stairs and ran down two stairwells, jumping the last couple of steps and skidding out onto the ground floor of the hospital. Women looked at him as he passed, but he didn't notice.

There was a store selling most things—mainly for visitors—and he grabbed lemon and raisin pancakes, a banana, chocolate and a snack pack of fresh strawberries, and headed back upstairs with his carrier bag full of goodies.

In the staffroom, Callie watched him thoughtfully as he arranged everything on a plate—slicing the banana and strawberries, pouring her a glass of milk and laying out the food as if it had been served at a hotel.

Then he turned to her with a smile, a towel folded over his arm as if he was a waiter. *'Voilà!'* he said with a flourish.

She laughed as she took it from him, and he grinned at her delight. Her laughter and pleasure made him feel good in a way he hadn't felt for some time. But Callie had always been able to cheer him up. She'd always been there for him. And there was something about her smile and childish delight that touched his heart.

'Now, you're not allowed to complain—in this situation I get to look after you,' he said.

Callie stabbed a strawberry with her fork and popped it into her mouth. 'I could get used to it.'

He nodded, his eyes shining with pleasure, and then a serious thought shot to the front of his head. It was a huge decision—a huge idea—but it felt so right and he just let it out.

'Then let me do it.'

'Do what?' she asked quizzically, another strawberry piece halfway to her mouth, suspended on the end of her fork.

'Move in with me. To the spare room,' he added, feeling his cheeks colour as he realised just what a huge thing he was asking.

Where had *that* idea come from? Okay, he hadn't liked the idea of not being there for every moment of her pregnancy, but he'd resigned himself to it. Hadn't he? It was what he would have had to do if Maggie had still been around. Or would it have come to this anyway? Her moving in to his spare room?

'No strings—nothing like that. Just a friend sleeping over. Just…let me look after you.' Suddenly he needed her to agree to this. And why not? They were best friends— how hard could it be? They'd spent years together, they knew each other inside out, and it wasn't romantic or anything. He knew that would never happen—she'd always been clear on that.

She slowly chewed the strawberry before swallowing. 'But why?'

'Because I shouldn't have to be worrying about you all the time!' His exasperation burst from him unexpectedly. 'I think about you constantly, Callie!' It was true. His mind was always on her just lately. Since the pregnancy, anyway. 'Whether you're okay, whether you're sick, if you're having pains, if you're bleeding and not saying anything. I worry, okay? It *is* natural—you *are* carrying my child.'

Callie stared at him, saying nothing. She wasn't used to people caring about her.

'I never wanted it to be this way.' He brought his voice down an octave or two, even though they were alone in the room. 'I thought I'd have a child the normal way, you know? Married…living with the woman who was carrying the baby…being there for everything. Missing nothing. The first kick. The first movement. The Braxton Hicks. The real contractions. The rush to hospital for the birth.' He let out a big sigh. 'I don't want to do this from a distance.'

'Do what?'

'*Fatherhood.* I can't do it from a distance, Callie. I'm not my father. At least consider it. Please?'

She stared long and hard at him and he wasn't sure whether to say any more. He decided to remain silent. He'd not meant to say *anything*! But it was tough, being a dad-to-be and not being allowed to hold the woman carrying your child. Not to be involved. He'd thought he'd be able to handle it, but what if he couldn't?

How had his own father done it? Eight kids in total, eight pregnancies, and he'd been away on duty in other countries for most of them. How had he got on with life? By not being there for it all? Easily. That was how. Because his father was a totally different creature. A man who liked to have the knowledge that his wife was forever pregnant, so other men knew she was taken, was unavailable, but without the day-to-day drudgery of being at home himself. He thought it was boring.

Callie was his best friend but the lines between them were blurring now, because of the baby she was carrying. She had always meant so much to him, but now she meant *everything*. She was precious and fragile and carrying his child—and he wanted to be there. Was that so wrong?

He couldn't think about what Maggie might have said if they'd still been together. How would she have reacted to him asking Callie to move in with them?

Not very well.

'I'll think about it,' she said, eating a slice of banana.

He nodded, satisfied with that answer for now. 'No strings. Strictly spare room stuff. Just…in the same home. That's all. Think of it as a long-term sleepover at a mate's house.'

Callie put down her fork as he reached out for her and wrapped his arms around her shoulders, holding her close, squeezing her gently, enjoying the feel of her next to him, knowing that this was as close as he would ever get.

'You worried me. I don't ever want to have to see you that vulnerable again,' he whispered into her hair. He felt her hot breath against the side of his head and realised he had to fight to not turn his face to her.

'I'm sorry.'

'Let me look after you. It'll be fun.'

She pulled back and looked at him, laughing. *'Fun?'*

It was good to laugh with her, to see the happiness in her eyes. 'Why not?'

Callie tilted her head to one side and looked at him strangely. 'I'd need to pay rent.'

He nodded. 'Fine.'

'And I'll do my own laundry.'

'Double fine.'

'And I get to cook sometimes.'

'Hmm…'

'Oy!' She gave him a prod. 'I'm not that bad!'

'Okay. Deal.' He held out his hand and she took it.

It had been a difficult time—a difficult event, seeing her collapse like that. But in these last few minutes he had his best friend back. And it felt good. Being close to her once again.

The only problem, Lucas began to realise as he sat facing her, was that he wasn't sure if he wanted to let go of her at all.

What mess had he got them both into?

CHAPTER THREE

CALLIE HAD MANAGED to get hold of Rhea on her mobile phone and persuaded her to come in. After Rhea had stormed off the other day there were still lots of things that Callie needed to do to make sure she was looking after Rhea in the best possible way. That meant doing blood tests and asking some of the questions that she hadn't got to ask in the first place.

As an incentive, she'd arranged for Rhea's first scan, hoping that the sight of her baby might make Rhea open up a bit more.

When she arrived, Callie noted that Rhea was wearing the same dowdy pink top and jeans as before, and was looking a little bedraggled. She invited her into the clinic room and offered her a cup of tea.

'I can't drink tea at the moment, thanks.'

'Me neither. Would you like coffee?'

Rhea looked at her, head tilted to one side. 'You're pregnant, too?'

'I am.' She smiled, hoping that this sharing of a confidence might provoke the same in her patient. 'Just out of that horrible first trimester. The sickness was awful—I tell you, it certainly made me think twice. How about you?'

Rhea nodded. 'I never wanted to be pregnant in the first place. The sickness was like extra punishment.'

Callie could empathise about the sickness. She smiled reassuringly. 'So the pregnancy is unplanned?'

'I didn't ask for it.' Rhea was instantly abrupt.

It was an odd response, and Callie wasn't sure what to make of it. 'What *did* you ask for?'

Again Rhea couldn't meet her eyes, but there were tears threatening again and Rhea was struggling to hold them back. Callie knew she had to offer Rhea something, in the hope that the girl would open up to her.

'Last time we met you mentioned you wanted to give the baby away. Have it adopted.'

'So?' The response was almost a challenge and Rhea glared at her, as if daring her to criticise.

'So…' Callie took a deep breath and plunged in. 'I want you to understand that adoption is a huge thing. It's difficult for the birth mother. You know…having carried the baby for nine months. Felt it kick, felt it move, gone through labour for it. I want to know that you've thought it all through.'

Callie didn't feel there was any need to mention that she was in a similar situation. For now, she needed Rhea to think hard about her choice, to look at her decision carefully. Without rushing.

Rhea looked at her with barely disguised curiosity. 'Yeah? I thought the Social would just take it away if I didn't want it.'

'Yes, they would. But they'd *also* give you the time to say goodbye. See the baby. Hold him or her. Some mothers who choose to have their babies adopted keep the baby for a few weeks, just to be sure of their decision.'

'I don't want to look after it! I don't want to see it!'

Callie frowned at such a strong, determined response. She wasn't judging Rhea's decision. She was free to make the choice to have her baby adopted. But Rhea was so young—only sixteen—and Callie knew she had to be sure that Rhea had thought this through properly and not just rushed into a decision because the pregnancy was still a shock.

'Okay, and that's fine—you don't have to if you don't want to. But, Rhea, you have to understand that, as a midwife, I know many women feel emotional after giving birth. It's such an arduous thing. It hurts, you're exhausted, but at the end of it—for most women—there's the prize, if you like, of a baby. They *need* to hold it. Need to see it. Smell it, touch it. See that after all those months of watching a bump grow their baby is real and that they're different people now. Mothers.'

'There's nothing you can say that will make me change my mind.'

Callie held up her hands. 'I'm not trying to. It's not my place and it would be totally unprofessional for anyone to do that. This is your choice, and whatever you choose will be fine by me.'

Rhea nodded firmly.

'As long as I know that you've thought through the consequences of your choice properly. It's not something you'll be able to just forget. It will always be with you.'

Rhea pulled her mobile phone from her pocket, checked the display and then put it away again. 'You're trying to make me feel guilty.'

'No. Absolutely not. But I *will* be devil's advocate and make sure you've thought through your choice—because, Rhea, you don't want to get a couple of years down the line and suddenly be filled with regret, with no way of reversing your decision.'

'You think I'll want it later on?' she scoffed. 'You've *got* to be kidding me.'

'I don't know how you'll feel later on. But I want you to think about it. I want you to imagine you give up this baby and a few years pass by, life carries on, and then you find yourself wondering about your daughter or your son.'

Rhea shook her head. 'I won't.'

'Okay, but I want you to think about it. You've got time, after all, if you're going to go through with the pregnancy.'

Rhea shrugged. 'I appreciate what you're doing, okay? You're a midwife. You must love babies to do this job. But I'm not you. I don't live in la-la land, where everything is right and beautiful. Where I come from it's tough and hard and life is cruel. I don't need to be saddled with the burden of a baby in a fourteenth-floor flat reached with a broken lift that stinks of old pee.'

'I know what it's like to have a tough life, Rhea. My childhood was no bed of roses, believe me.'

Callie bit her lip. This wasn't the time to be sharing personal information with Rhea. It wasn't professional. But she needed to get through to her somehow.

'Let me guess...your parents got you the wrong type of doll?'

'Actually, my alcoholic mother dragged me through childhood. Reluctantly.'

She regretted her words as soon as she'd said them. Callie knew better than to share that much personal information with a patient. But there was something about this young girl that called out to her.

Rhea stared hard at Callie, assessing her words, judging if she thought they were real. But she must have seen the truth in Callie's eyes, because she looked away and then apologised.

'It's okay. I'm sorry. I should never have said that.' Callie told her.

'I'm glad you did. Made you seem a bit more real.'

'Worldly-wise?' Callie smiled.

Rhea managed a small smile, the corners of her mouth turning up. 'Yeah.'

'It's easy to assume that everyone else's life is better than ours, but sometimes it just isn't.'

'No.'

Callie gathered the notes on her desk, taking a deep breath, and changed the subject slightly. 'Do you have support, Rhea? Family?'

'My mum—though she's as much use as a chocolate chisel.'

Callie smiled. Snap. Her own mother was now supposedly a *recovered* alcoholic, rather than an 'active' one, but Callie wasn't sure whether she was or not. Maria *said* she was off the sauce, but Maria was a born liar and Callie had heard enough lies to last a lifetime.

It was the one thing she couldn't stand more than anything. Liars. There was just something so horrible about them. Being untruthful. Taking you for a fool. Not respecting you enough to give you the truth. Assuming you were stupid enough to fall for the fallacy. Everything Callie's mother now said she took with a pinch of salt.

It was why she tried her hardest to have as little to do with her as she could, despite Maria's constant efforts to get in touch. The times Callie *had* bothered, the times she had made the effort, had always been in vain and dealing with the constant let-downs was just getting too much. It was easier not to try.

'Your dad? Brothers? Sisters?'

'Just mum.'

Like me. And Rhea is pregnant—like me. And both our mothers are useless and both of us are pregnant in difficult circumstances.

Tears began to prick and burn her eyes and she quickly turned away, pretending to look for something in a drawer. She felt a tap on her arm and turned back to see that Rhea was holding a box of tissues out to her. The box of tissues that Callie usually offered her patients, only now the situation was reversed.

'It's okay,' Rhea said softly. 'These hormones make you crazy, don't they?'

Callie half laughed, half cried and, nodding, she took a tissue.

What is the matter with me?

'Sorry, Rhea. This is very unprofessional.'

'Don't be. I should be the one saying sorry. I was being harsh.'

'But if you have reason to be—'

'There was no need for me to be rude. You were trying to help.'

Callie nodded, sniffing, and dabbed at her nose with the tissue. Letting out a breath, she relaxed her shoulders, sat forward and laid a hand on Rhea's knee. 'How are you coping?'

'I'm okay.'

'Are you doing this alone? Is the father in the picture?'

She couldn't help but think of Lucas, the father of her own baby. She'd agreed to move in with him! Would she regret that? Had *she* made a decision without thinking it through? What would it be like, living with Lucas for all those months, only to move out when the baby was born? Would he even want her there?

Of course not. It's the baby he's after. I'm his friend, but that's all. This was always about giving Lucas the baby— nothing's changed.

The thoughts made her feel sad again, but she bit the inside of her lip and tried to concentrate on that rather than allow herself to cry again. She'd already embarrassed herself once today...

'I need a biscuit. Something with chocolate. You?'

'Yes, please. I'm ravenous.'

'Are you eating properly?' Callie got a packet of chocolate chip cookies from her drawer and opened them, offering them to Rhea, who took three.

'I haven't got much money.'

'But you live with your mother?'

Rhea nodded.

'Does she cook for you?'

'She isn't in often.'

No. Callie knew what *that* was like. She'd lost count of the amount of times she'd come home from school to find nothing in the house but empty beer cans or discarded bottles. Plenty of empties, but not much else. She recalled one dinner time when the only thing she'd been able to find in the cupboards was an old tin of custard powder. She'd made herself custard for lunch, just to have something hot before she went back to school for the afternoon.

Callie shook her head. 'My mother was never the best.'

Rhea shrugged. 'But I bet *you'll* be.'

'Rhea! Are you trying to tell me I'd make a good mother?'

'Sure. You're a midwife. You're caring. How much better could you be?'

How about how wrong could I be? What about being in a committed relationship? Raising a child together?

But it was the first time Callie had seen Rhea smile. Properly, anyway. Perhaps they'd made a connection after all?

She laughed, thinking of Lucas. His blue eyes and the way he looked at her. The way his dark hair always looked tousled, no matter how much he combed it. The way he made her *feel*. Before all of this Lucas had been her best friend and, yes, she loved him. *As a friend.* But her pregnancy was changing things. Her hormones were changing things. Maggie leaving had changed everything and it was all up in the air now.

Callie didn't know what to think. What to feel. Before Maggie had left it had all been straightforward. Get pregnant, have the baby, give it to Maggie and Lucas and then play doting godparent or something. But now…?

'I shouldn't have told you any of that, you know. Not very professional.' She wiped her eyes dry and smiled.

Rhea nodded, seeming to be thinking deeply. Then she took a deep breath and said, 'My mum's thrown me out.'

Callie was shocked. She'd not been expecting that. 'Oh, Rhea…'

'I'm sleeping on a friend's couch. Have been for a week or two.'

'She knows about the pregnancy? That's why she threw you out?'

Rhea nodded and grabbed a tissue from the box for herself. 'She thinks I'm a tart. That I got pregnant deliberately, that it's all my fault. And it wasn't! It *wasn't*…'

Callie offered fresh tissues. 'What happened? Will you tell me?'

Rhea met her gaze and eventually nodded. 'I was at a party. At a friend's house. There was alcohol and I'd never really tried it before, so I think it went to my head quite quickly. I went to lay down in her room—try and sleep it off because I felt awful. I woke up in the dark and there was someone on top of me. I tried to stop him. I really tried. But he was stronger than me…' She sounded so matter-of-fact.

Callie stared on in horror. 'You were *raped*?'

'Mum reckons I asked for it. She's disgusted with me.'

'Did you go to the police?'

'Yes. But I'd already had a shower and they reckoned I'd washed away a lot of the evidence.'

'Oh, Rhea, I'm so sorry! Did they test you for STIs?'

'They came back negative.'

'But you were pregnant?'

'Yes. That's why I want to get rid of it.'

Callie could now understand why Rhea had been so up-tight, so resistant to her prying questions. She felt glad now that she'd confided in Rhea herself, because it had shown Rhea that Callie could be trusted.

'That's why you don't want to keep it?'

Rhea shook her head. 'How could I? Every time I looked at it I'd be reminded. I'd see its eyes looking at me and—'

'And it would love you. The child. The baby would have no idea about its conception. It would just see you as its mother. It would *love* you.'

Rhea shook her head, violently disagreeing. 'No.'

Callie sat silently for a moment. They'd both shared an awful lot. She'd said something herself that she'd not meant to say. Certainly not to a patient. Even if it *had* been to get Rhea to open up and trust her.

'Let me arrange some counselling for you.'

'I don't need it.'

'It can help to have someone to talk to.'

'I've got you.'

Callie nodded. 'Okay. But I'll need to take some blood from you today. I should have done it last time.'

'What for?'

'To check your blood group. Check your rhesus status—that sort of thing.'

People could be either rhesus positive or rhesus negative, depending on their blood type.

'Right. I see.'

'I've booked you in for a scan as well. We need to do certain checks on the baby—check its growth and health. It's an ultrasound. Will you do it?'

'Do I have to look at it?'

'Not if you don't want to. But aren't you curious to see it?'

'No. I don't want to get attached to it.'

The walls had gone up again.

'In case it makes it harder to give away?'

Rhea met her gaze, nodded, and quickly looked away.

Callie could understand her reasons.

Rhea lay down on the same couch that Callie had just a few days ago and had gel smeared onto her abdomen. The sonographer spent a few moments getting her bearings and then turned to look at Callie, who was sitting in. 'Well, everything looks just fine.'

Callie reached for Rhea's hand and squeezed it. 'Do you want to see?'

'But if I see it—'

'Rhea...please...let me turn the screen. You need to see this.'

The teenager gave in and nodded, the expression on her face turning from a mix of apprehension and fear to one of confusion and wonder. 'What is that?'

Callie wasn't sure whether to smile or not. 'That's your baby.'

How would Rhea react? What would she feel?

At her own scan Callie had felt awe and a little afraid, if she were honest with herself. The pregnancy was *real*. No longer a hypothetical situation.

Rhea would have no choice now but to face facts.

Lucas sucked in a breath, then sighed heavily down the phone. 'I've asked Callie to move in with me.' He waited for the reaction from his mother, not knowing how she'd be.

'Right. Well, that makes sense.'

She still didn't sound too pleased, but then again she hadn't been happy with him ever since he'd mentioned the divorce and the surrogacy.

'And how's she doing?'

'Callie's doing well. She was a little faint at work the other day, so I suggested she move in so that I can look after her.'

'And that's all this is?'

He rubbed his forehead roughly. What *was* it with everyone suggesting there was more to their relationship?

'Yes! She's just my friend. There's nothing untoward about this.'

'Moving in together is a big deal, Lucas. You two have known each other for years and I know how you felt about her once and what it did to you when she turned you down. Are you sure there's nothing else going on?'

'Mum—'

'Maggie never liked her, did she? Always suspected your friendship was more than that?'

His mother was right. Maggie had never liked Callie very much. Or his friendship with her. It had been a difficult line he'd had to walk when he'd still been married to Maggie. Every phone call or conversation with Callie had had to be explained in minute detail, as if she'd suspected him of wanting to jump into bed with Callie at any moment.

Maybe once he'd wanted that, but they'd both been very young then. He'd adored Callie. Had been able to picture them both together as a couple and been excited to think that she'd say yes.

When he'd asked her and she'd got all upset before telling him no, they could never be together that way...*ever*...his heart had been broken. Never had he imagined that she'd turn him down. So he'd gone straight out and at the first club he'd gone into he'd met Maggie and bought her a drink.

Maggie—whom he'd treated appallingly by trying too hard to love her. Forcing feelings that had never been true...

Callie wouldn't risk their friendship back then and she sure as hell wouldn't now! So his mother had nothing to worry about. He knew where he stood with Callie. It had been clear then and it was clear now.

'Well, Maggie's not here anymore, is she? It doesn't matter. Callie and I are friends. I just thought I'd let you know what was happening.'

There was a pause. 'I see. And have you decided what's going to happen when the baby's born? Does she move out then?'

Lucas refused even to think that far. He certainly didn't like the idea of thinking of her moving out before he'd even got her moved in! 'I don't know.' He knew he didn't like the idea of her leaving.

'Well, you need to decide. Before that poor baby is born.'

'My child is not a "poor baby". It will be cherished and adored. You've no need to feel sorry for it.'

'Of *course* I feel sorry for it. It might never have a mother.' She sighed. 'Why didn't you marry Callie in the first place? You know that's what your father and I wanted for you.'

Lucas gritted his teeth. Of course he knew. Because he and Callie had been friends for so long they'd always hinted at it, or joked about it, but he'd seen the look on Callie's face every time they did. Shock…fear. Didn't they know that it had killed him to see her look that way? Didn't they know that it had destroyed him to know he couldn't have her? That she'd never contemplate it?

He refused to lose his temper. There was no point in going over old ground. Callie would never look at him in that way.

Ever.

Callie opened up the suitcase on her bed and stared at her clothes hanging in the wardrobe. She was meant to be packing. Getting ready for moving in with Lucas—just whilst she was pregnant—so that he could be there for her and the baby.

There's nothing romantic about this, so why do I feel so strange? So nervous?

She didn't want to call her mother—Maria was usually the last person she turned to—but she needed to talk to someone and it couldn't be Lucas. After her time spent discussing what had happened with Rhea, she felt as if she needed the connection that family gave. Even if Maria *was* useless, she could still be a sounding board—so she picked up the phone and dialled.

It rang for a long time, and just when she thought her mother must be out or in a drunken stupor somewhere it was answered.

'Yes?'

'Mum? It's me—Callie.'

'Oh, hi. I thought you might be someone else.' As always, her mother's regret at being connected to Callie shone through.

'Sorry. I can go if you're waiting for another call.'

'No, it's fine. I'm glad you rang. I've been wanting to speak to you.'

Well, then, you could have called me, couldn't you? Busy getting to the bottom of a bottle?

'I just wanted to talk…speak to you…let you know that…um…I'm having a baby. I'm pregnant.'

There was silence at the other end of the phone for a moment, though Callie felt sure she heard the slosh of a bottle being upended.

'A baby? Congratulations.'

Maria didn't sound thrilled. But what had Callie expected?

'I didn't even know you were in a relationship.'

You never called to find out.

She closed her eyes with dismay and hurt. What had she really expected from her? Support? Happiness? Joy at becoming a grandmother?

Who was I kidding?

'No, no, I'm not. I…er…just thought I'd tell you that you won't be able to get hold of me at this number for a while.'

'Oh?'

'I'm going to be moving in with the father… It's Lucas, by the way. This is his number, if you want to contact me there.' She read off the number, knowing in her heart that her mother would not be writing it down.

'You and Lucas? That's great. I always thought you two would end up together.'

It was too complicated to explain. 'Okay. I guess that's it. Take care.'

'Callie, wait!'

'Yes?' *What now?*

'He's been your best friend, hasn't he, all these years? I guess it was to be expected you'd have a baby with him.'

'Well, it's not straightforward.'

'What is in this life? Well, I'm happy for you both. I have some news too.'

'Yes?'

'I've met someone. Someone special to me. His name's Gareth and I'd like you to meet him.'

Callie had lost count of the number of 'someone specials' she'd had to meet over the years. This Gareth would surely be just another man in the long list of men that her mother hung around with—hangers-on, fellow drunks. She wasn't desperate to meet him at all.

'Well, I'm very busy at work.'

'Oh, I see.' Her mother sounded disappointed.

'I'll try to come over soon, I'm just not sure when.'

'Things are different now, Callie. I've changed. Gareth's helped me change. I haven't had a drink for six months.'

Lies. All lies!

Callie had heard all this before! She almost couldn't bear it—the way her mother handed out the same old patter all the time! Expecting her to believe it!

What sort of a fool does she take me for?

'Really? Well…keep it up.'

'I will. I *am*. I mean it this time, Callie. I really do.'

'I hope so. But you've said all this before, Mum.'

'I know I have, and I know it's difficult for you to believe me, but this time I'll prove it. In actions *and* words.'

Callie couldn't speak. There was too much emotion flowing through her at that moment. If she did speak, she'd cry.

'So I'll look forward to seeing you soon?'

She sucked in a deep breath and gathered herself. 'Sure. Bye.'

Callie put the phone down and shook her head at her own stupidity.

What was I thinking? She isn't going to care about a grandchild! She could barely care about her own *child! She hardly said anything when I said I was pregnant. She cares more about this Gareth person!*

'She's still drinking,' she announced to the empty room, to her empty suitcase, and she began to well up, then cry, as she pulled her clothes from the wardrobe and shoved them haphazardly into her suitcase.

Lucas would be round soon. He'd said he would be there about five to pick her up and take her to his.

It had been a long time since she'd last been at his place. She'd liked it there. It was safe. Homely. Not like her own. It would be nice to come home from work and not find an empty flat. There'd be someone to talk to. Someone to share her day with. They could each get exasperated about work and know where the other one was coming from.

Like a couple.

Now where had *that* thought come from?

Wiping her eyes, she sat down on the bed and thought about him. Did she like Lucas? In *that* way?

He is gorgeous. Kind and funny and caring and...yes, okay, he's hot.

But he was a friend. A friend she was now having a baby

with. Moving in with until it was born. She couldn't risk losing his friendship by having romantic feelings for him!

I'm not feeling that way. I'm not! It's just hormones, that's all.

Will I have to move out when the baby's born?

They hadn't spoken about it. She hadn't asked. But now she needed to know. What *did* Lucas expect of her after the birth? Anything? The original plan had been that she would be like an aunt, or a godmother or something. She'd be in the baby's life but on the edges, the fringe. *Maggie* was meant to have been the mother, but she'd gone now.

Does Lucas want me to be the baby's mother?

She knew she'd have to ask him. This was too big a deal not to get cleared up, too big a question not to ask. She couldn't assume. She'd have to ask him.

But what do I want to hear? I've never wanted to be a mother. But I know I want the best for this child.

She folded her jeans and placed them into her suitcase, absentmindedly laying a couple of reading books in the suitcase, a small toiletries case, a camera.

The clock said five past five when the doorbell rang.

It's him.

She got up and checked her reflection in the mirror. 'Bad hair, red eyes, chafed cheeks. I look great,' she muttered, and headed for the front door.

When she opened it she saw him take one look at her and read her face, but instead of the joke that she was expecting about how awful she looked he simply dropped the bouquet of flowers he was holding and pulled her into his arms, crushing her against his broad chest. He squeezed her tight and she could feel his lips in her hair, kissing the top of her head, whilst she inhaled his heavenly scent as if he was oozing pure amber nectar.

'What's wrong? Has someone upset you?'

She could hear his heart pounding through his strong

chest and it felt good to stand there, wrapped in his embrace, protected and warm and safe. He smelt amazing, and it would have been so easy just to stand there and let him hold her and never let go. So easy just to melt into him and stay there. Never moving, never letting go.

'I spoke to my mum...' she mumbled into his shirt. 'You know what she's like.' She pulled away, smiling sheepishly, and tucked a stray strand of hair behind her ear.

He walked with her into the flat, closing the door behind them. 'You told her?'

With reluctance, she nodded and sat down on the couch opposite. 'Yep. She reacted pretty much how I expected. You'll probably be pleased to know there'll be no pushy grandma from *my* side of the family.' She smiled, but the smile didn't reach her eyes. Then, as an afterthought, she asked, 'Were those flowers for me?'

'Dammit!' He leapt over the couch in one fluid movement and went back outside, picking up the flowers he'd dropped. Brushing off imaginary fluff, he presented them to her. They were beautiful! Lots of tiny pink roses, mostly still in bud. 'Flat-warming. I thought you could put them in your new bedroom.'

She lifted them to her nose and inhaled their delicate scent. 'They're lovely—thank you. You always know how to make me feel better.'

Lucas smiled. 'I try. So what did Maria say, exactly?'

'Well, I got a "congratulations" but she was too busy telling me about her new man to offer anything else.' Callie fiddled with the pink roses. 'She wants me to meet him.'

'But you don't want to?'

'I've met too many of her men. Oh, and she saw fit to inform me she's been off the booze for six months.'

'That's good, isn't it?'

'It'll be a lie.'

Lucas looked grim. 'Maybe, but what if she is telling the truth?'

Callie looked at him in disbelief and laughed. 'Hardly!'

Lucas persisted. 'But if she *is*...don't you think you should give her that chance? She's your mother. That's not a relationship you can just ignore.'

'Why not? She's done a good job of it for all these years. Why do I have to be the responsible one?'

He shrugged. 'Because you're about to be a mother yourself?'

There. He'd said it. But Callie still didn't know if she *was* going to be a mother, did she? Lucas and she hadn't discussed, yet, just exactly what her role was going to be now.

We need to clear this up soon.

'I think you ought to go and visit her. See for yourself.'

'I don't see the point, Lucas.'

'She's your *mum*.'

'Yes. She is. But only in title. I've always had to look after myself.' Her answer was final, suggesting the conversation was over where Maria was concerned.

Lucas let out a big sigh and looked around. 'Is there anything you need help with? Or are you already packed?' He was eyeing her flat, and she had to admit it didn't look as if she'd packed much.

'It's pretty much done. I was just finishing my suitcase when you rang.'

'So you're still happy to move in?'

She nodded. 'If you're happy—though I think there are a few things we still need to talk about.'

'I agree. But we've plenty of time to iron out the wrinkles in this situation. Let's not rush into making life-changing decisions straight away.'

She was glad to hear that he must have been thinking things through, too. 'Okay, so let's start with an easy one. Who's cooking tonight?'

He laughed and she smiled at the sound, enjoying the way his eyes twinkled with merriment. Glad that they were back on easier territory. Lucas had always tried to get her to be closer to her mother. Probably because he had a close relationship with his own mother. Well, he was lucky. Not everyone had that.

'Someone else will… I thought we could make it special. Our first meal together. At a nice restaurant… Because I'm damned sure I'm not going to have a baby with someone who I haven't taken out to dinner.'

It had been ages since she'd last been there, but his flat was exactly as she remembered. There'd once been a time when she'd felt she could pop round whenever she needed to, but when Lucas had got together with Maggie that freedom to visit had ended. She and Maggie had got on okay, but there had been a sense of 'stay away' that she'd got from Maggie when it came to visiting. Almost as if Maggie was laying claim to Lucas—especially after she'd married him.

Lucas had always told Callie to come round, but she hadn't called in as often as she'd used to, and she'd always made up some excuse. There was no way she would have caused problems in his marriage with Maggie.

But now she was looking forward to reclaiming her friendship with him. Regaining the closeness they'd once had.

All the photos that had once been there of him and Maggie were gone. Thankfully. It would have been disturbing if they'd still been there. At least it showed that he didn't still need her picture about, reminding him of their shared past.

Lucas gave her a quick tour, though she pretty much already knew where most things were. But she hadn't seen the spare room before. It was bigger than she'd realised, and decorated in a beautiful pale blue. A large double bed dominated the centre of the room, covered in a gorgeous crocheted creamy-white throw.

Callie raised an eyebrow at this, looking for Lucas to explain. It seemed a very girly decoration.

'Before you say anything, I bought that for you. Maggie took all the pretty covers we'd bought and left me with my old black and grey ones, and my inner interior designer made me go out and get something a little more feminine.' He grinned and heaved her suitcase into the room before depositing it on the bed. 'Want a hand to unpack?'

'I'm all right, thanks.'

'Okay. Dinner reservations are for seven-thirty.'

'Where are we going?'

'Gianni's. It's Italian—I'm sure you said you liked that once.'

She smiled. He'd remembered. 'I love Italian.'

'Great. I'll leave you to it, then.'

'Are we getting dressed up?'

He hovered in the doorway, his hands casually in his pockets. 'We can do. Might be nice. We *are* celebrating.'

'Okay.'

It would be nice to get dressed up, and she hadn't been out to eat for ages! Two months' worth of morning sickness had put paid to any appetite she'd had, but that was gone now. Callie was feeling much better, and she finally understood why some of her women were so glad to get that first trimester out of the way!

'Wow…you look…*amazing*.'

Lucas couldn't believe his eyes. Callie was wearing a gorgeous figure-hugging dress, all red and flowing, close-fitting at the hips and loose around her legs.

And what a pair of legs! Her calves were shapely and toned—and he wasn't sure why he was so surprised.

I guess I'm so used to seeing her in scrubs.

She'd obviously been keeping her figure a secret beneath the shapeless hospital garb. But there was a lovely gentle rounding around her abdomen, and he knew it was caused by the fundus of her womb spilling over the pelvic cavity and rising up as it swelled in size.

My baby.

She looked great. Blooming and healthy and...

Gorgeous!

There was no other word for it. She'd done her hair and put on make-up and he couldn't recall ever seeing her looking like this! She was glowing! As she smiled shyly at his response, her cheeks flushing, he had to fight the desire to reach out and stroke her cheek.

What's that all about?

He cleared his throat, trying to tamp down the physical response his body was having to her sensual curves.

She'd done something to her hair, too, curling it, sweeping it up, but letting small pieces hang down here and there. She looked tousled—as if she'd just had a good session in bed!

Calm yourself, Lucas, this is Callie...

Yes. It most certainly was Callie. She'd always been pretty, though she'd never played up to it as far as he could recall. But for some reason looking at her tonight, right now, she was more than just a pretty friend...she was beautiful and alluring...

'Wow...' he repeated.

'Thanks. You don't scrub up too badly yourself.'

He'd put on a dinner jacket and white shirt, though he hadn't bothered with a tie. His suit was tailored and well-fitting, and he was glad he'd put it on after seeing the effort she'd gone to.

Escorting her down to his car, he held the door open for her and waited for her to get in. He tried not to take advantage of his position, but he couldn't help getting a good view of her legs again and inhaling the scent of her perfume. He took a deep breath to try and regain control of his raging senses as he walked to his side of the car and then drove to Gianni's. He felt as if he was on a proper date.

Gianni's was a small Italian restaurant on the edge of London. It had had some excellent reviews by restaurant critics and he'd been there once before with some friends. Inside, it was dimly lit by wall sconces and individual candles on each of the tables, and a guy at a real piano played soft background music. No schmaltzy taped music here!

'Wow, this place is gorgeous,' Callie said.

'I'm glad you like it.' They went up to the maître d', who was waiting by a desk. 'Table for two under the name Gold.'

'Certainly, sir. This way, please.'

The maître d' led them to a small table for two, situated at the back of the restaurant. French doors near their table opened out onto a balcony, covered with bougainvillaea and filled with pots of flowers and a small water fountain. The view looked out over the lights of London.

'This place is amazing, Lucas,' Callie said in awe, draping her wrap over the back of her chair as he held it out for her.

He tried not to smell her hair as she stood before him, and he really struggled to keep his hands off her. He felt guilty. Maggie's words were haunting him.

When she was seated he quickly settled himself into his own chair opposite, glad to put some physical distance between them. Seeing her all done up like this was great and all, but…it was making him think crazy things! This was *Callie*! Not a date. Nothing romantic. But, by God, she was doing something crazy to his insides…

'I'm glad you like it.'

Callie wouldn't drink any wine, so they ordered soft drinks whilst they perused the menu. Lucas couldn't help but sneak peeks at her over his own menu whilst he pretended to read, and his stomach was in knots with nerves. He had to break the tension he felt inside, so he laid his menu down to reach across the table and take her hand.

He stared at her fingers within his own and played with one of her rings, pondering his question for a moment. Then he looked up at her and said, 'I've always meant to ask you something.'

She looked slightly afraid, worried about what he'd ask. 'Oh…?'

'Yes…it's something I've been meaning to ask you for a long time.'

'Yes?' Her breath sounded as if it was caught in her throat. What did she think he was going to ask?

He paused for a moment, dragging the tension out. 'What's Callie short for? Is it Calista? Something like that? In all these years we've known each other you've never said.'

She laughed with visible relief, squeezing his fingers and shaking her head as if in disbelief. '*That* was your big question?'

'That was my big question. For now.' He grinned.

'It's not Calista.'

'No?'

'No. And you don't really want to know what it's short for. There's a reason I've never told you, you know.'

'Is it something weird? Like Caligula? Be honest with me—are you named after a Roman emperor?'

They both laughed, and she took a sip of fruit juice before answering. 'I don't know why I've never told you. Actually, I *do* know—it's because I'd be embarrassed.' She took a deep breath. 'Promise me you won't laugh if I do.'

'I promise.' He mimed crossing his heart across his chest and smiled at her, loving the way she looked, so soft and gentle in the candlelight.

She looked at him carefully, weighing up his promise. 'You know what my mother was like, right?'

'Yes.'

'A drunk…an alcoholic. She never wanted me. Hardly bothered to acknowledge me sometimes. So she didn't even bother thinking of a name for me when I was born. *But*… she had to register me. Obviously she needed the child benefit money for drinking. So she went to the register office and when they asked her for my name…'

He was listening intently, wondering about the possible outcome.

'She looked about the room for the first thing she saw. There was a calendar on the wall and so she called me… Calendar. Calendar Taylor.'

Lucas didn't laugh. He'd promised. And there was something so inherently sad about the story that it didn't seem the slightest bit amusing now. He'd hoped it would be something exotic—Calliope, or something like that—something interesting. But instead it was simply a very sad story about a mother who seemed to care nothing for her child.

'I'm so sorry.' He reached out and tightened his grip around her fingers once again. He realised that he suddenly wanted to kiss her. Kiss her madly to take away the sadness and the pain that she'd experienced over the years at the hands of her mother. Crush her against his body, his lips to hers, with so much passion that neither of them would be able to breathe until it was all over and they had to break apart for air. Kiss her the way a lover might…

A lover?

The realisation startled him, so instead of holding her tightly he let her hand go. He took a sip from his drink, feeling the condensation on the glass, the drops of water, giving himself a chance to cool down. There was no way *that* was going to happen. Not with Callie. He knew that.

When he felt he might have control over his voice box he called the waiter over so they could order.

Callie had told him what she'd like and he ordered for them both: pan-fried tiger prawns in butter and chilli for a starter, *agnello* for main—which was a braised lamb shank in tomatoes and a red berry jus. When the first course arrived he heard her apologise. 'Sorry if I've ruined the evening. Mentioning my mother does that a lot.'

'I always knew you and your mother didn't get along. That she was an alcoholic. But I guess if you never have high expectations of her she can't let you down.'

'I suppose.'

'But, you know, even normal families have their issues.'

'Really? Are you trying to cheer me up?'

He smiled at her over the candlelight. 'I am. Both my parents were sober, but I had six sisters! Being the seventh child and the long-awaited son, in a family whose father was always absent for one reason or another, didn't always make for a great time either.'

'But you were the only boy. They'd wanted a son all that time. You *have* to admit you were a little spoilt!' She smiled to show she was joking.

'Are you kidding me? I had to fight for any attention that came my way. Positive attention was rare and negative was in great supply. My father, when he was there, was always quite happy to use his belt and make me into a man. My parents had all these dreams for me and they pushed me hard. *Very* hard. Sometimes nothing I did was right. All my life they'd wanted me to be a doctor and so that's what I became—just so they would be proud of me. I sometimes wonder what I might have been if they hadn't steered me in that direction.'

Callie frowned. 'But you love being a doctor, don't you?'

He nodded. 'Absolutely. I *do* love it. But that's just luck, isn't it? My parents wanted the best for me—a career, mar-

riage with children—but only when the time was right…
when my career had taken off. They didn't like Maggie,
they didn't like me choosing to marry her, and they let me
know about it.'

'How?'

'They initially told me they wouldn't come to the wedding. That I was making a mistake.' He chose not to explain
that his parents had actually told him he was marrying the
wrong woman and that *Callie* should have been the one in
a veil. 'And look at how *that* turned out. They were right.'

He sipped at his drink.

'You rushed into the marriage?'

'Maybe. You turned me down!' He laughed to lighten
the atmosphere, not referencing the great pain in his heart
at the memory. 'So I had to look elsewhere. I met Maggie
and down the aisle we went, without thinking about what
we were doing until it was too late. I should have waited,
maybe, but I thought I knew what I was doing. I was never
in love with Maggie. Not the way I should have been. I see
that now.'

Callie was listening intently, her heart saddened by these
revelations. She should have known about this, but hadn't
because she'd been so wrapped up in her own problems.
'I never realised.'

'Why would you?'

'Well, I'm your best friend. Perhaps I should have known
instinctively? Perhaps you should have felt able to tell me?'

'Neither of us are psychic, Callie. You had too much
going on in your own life to be worrying about mine. I
didn't want to burden you. At the time all this was happening your mum was in hospital with that liver complaint.'

'I do feel like maybe I let you down, though. You should
have been able to talk to me about it.'

But he knew that he wouldn't have. Why would he?
He'd had those intense feelings for Callie, which had slowly

developed over time, without him realising, and when he'd finally discovered the nerve to ask her out she'd turned him down! He'd been heartbroken. In all his imaginings he'd never expected her to say no. The let-down had been devastating and he'd reacted by going out to a club. That was when he had run into Maggie.

'People make you hurt,' she said with understanding.

Once again, she'd hit the nail on the head. She'd always understood him so well. 'I guess both of us would have changed things if we could.'

'Oh, I don't know. If my mother hadn't been the way she was then I might never have become a midwife.' She looked up and smiled. 'And we get to work together.'

'I love that we're still together. After all this time. So many people lose their childhood friends when they become adults. Move apart.'

'I'm glad too.' She looked into his eyes. 'I would like to discuss our situation, though, Lucas. We've got a lot to sort out, you and me.'

'I know.'

But he was afraid of letting her down. He'd let Maggie down by treating her badly, by not loving her the way he should have and driving her into the arms of another man. No wonder she'd gone looking for love elsewhere if she'd thought that he loved Callie. What woman would stand for that?

He'd tried so hard to make his marriage work, to make Maggie happy, to give her the child she wanted so badly— but he'd been doing it all for the wrong reasons. His heart had always been with Callie, even though he knew nothing could come of it.

Maggie had been right to leave him.

For a while they ate in companionable silence. The food was delicious—not too rich, yet full of flavour, with explosions of taste on their tongues.

'What we're doing…it's a big thing,' she said.

Lucas put down his knife and fork and dabbed at his mouth with his napkin. 'Moving in together?'

'The baby. It seemed a simple thing for me when Maggie was still going to be the mother, but she's gone now and I can't help but wonder…' She looked down at her lap, almost afraid to say her next words.

He waited for her to finish, but it seemed she couldn't say what she wanted to say. He leaned forward, looking past the candles, past the small posy of flowers on the table and deep into her eyes.

'I'd like you to be involved,' he said softly. 'As much as you'd like.' He paused for a moment before continuing. 'Actually, that's not true. I want you to be involved a hundred per cent. I know you've always said that you've never wanted to be a mother, but…'

'I never felt I could be what a child would need me to be.'

'But why not?'

He could see her eyes filling up. She was trying her hardest to blink away the tears, but couldn't stop a solitary tear from rolling down her cheeks.

He hated that she was upset. That she was hurting.

'I just…I wouldn't know *how* to be a mother.'

'Does anyone?'

'It should be instinctive. I never had that instinct. Never felt it. Never experienced it.' The tears trickled freely down her cheeks now 'Damn…I'm always crying just lately.'

He reached out with his napkin and dabbed at her cheek. There was so much he should be saying to her. That she still looked beautiful even if she was crying. But instead he went with, 'It's hormones. You can't help it.'

She hiccupped a laugh.

The waiter came and took away their starter plates and they sat quietly at the table. Lucas held her hand. How could he not? He didn't want to see her upset or crying, but he knew she must be scared because he was too. Every time he touched her now it was getting harder and harder to let her go. They'd always been close, but now that she was carrying his baby…

Moving in together, although it was just as room-mates, *was* a big deal. He was welcoming Callie into his life so that he could be there for them both, and he hoped that by doing so she would become happy and feel safe.

He knew she didn't want to be a mother. Was scared about being a mother. It was why she'd sworn off children. But she'd become a midwife—a profession where caring for others was tantamount. Could she not see that? She was one of the most caring people he knew and he felt instinctively, even if she didn't, that she would be a great mother. He knew she could be if she gave herself that chance.

He wanted his child to have a mother like Callie. For Callie to consider herself to be its mother. All his life he'd insisted that whenever he had a child it would be in a stable relationship, hopefully he'd be married, but whatever the situation it had to be stable and strong and definitely with a mother as well as a father. Parents who were around for their kids every day.

It was something he hadn't had with his own father. And when his father *had* been around he'd been angry and had had little patience with a young boy who'd craved his approval… There'd be no getting out the belt for *his* child. His and Callie's baby.

Would Callie agree to be that parent?

He wouldn't ask anything of her apart from that. There'd be no demands on them to become an actual couple. They didn't have to start 'going out'. She'd already turned him down once before and he knew she wouldn't let that happen anyway. It was totally out of the question for her. Wasn't it? And he could keep his feelings separate. Somehow. Callie could be a mother without being his partner. Although…

I wouldn't stop it. I think Callie and me would be good together. I always have.

But he knew he couldn't press her that way. She'd turn tail and run for it—as she had before when he'd tried to ask her out. That had been years ago now, and she hadn't wanted to risk their friendship. But things were different now, weren't they? They were both adults, for a start, and they knew what they were doing. Supposedly.

Their lamb shanks arrived and they tucked in with gusto. The meat was tender and just melted in the mouth. The green beans were perfectly *al dente* and the potatoes soft and full of flavour, with butter and mint melting over them.

They kept the conversation neutral for the rest of the evening. One set of tears had been enough for them both and Lucas didn't want to upset Callie any more about anything. They talked about films they'd both seen, which led to Callie announcing that a new documentary about midwifery was going to start on television and she wanted to see it.

'Should be interesting. It's meant to be real-life fly-on-the-wall stuff.'

'Could you imagine if they filmed in *our* hospital?'

She laughed. 'Oh, my God! That would be priceless!'

Their puddings came and went, the evening rolled on pleasantly, and much too soon it was time for home.

When they got back to the flat Callie kicked off her heels and stumbled onto the couch. 'I'm beat.'

'What shift are you on tomorrow?' Lucas asked.

'I've got three night shifts in a row. You?'

'A late shift tomorrow, then two nights.'

'I guess we'll run into each other, then.'

'Guess so.'

They were staring at each other. Uncomfortably so. As if each of them was expecting the other to say something or do something definitive.

But when Lucas didn't make a move Callie stood up

with a sigh and went to pick up her heels, then she turned to walk to her room. 'I'm going to bed. Thanks for tonight. It was lovely.'

Lucas stood up and nodded. 'It was my pleasure.'

She looked at him from across the room. Was there tension between them? Sexual tension?

She walked over to give him a friendly peck on the cheek, her lips caressing rough stubble. 'Good night.' She paused again, as if she was thinking of something, but then smiled and turned away before he could process it too much.

'Goodnight, Callie.'

He watched her go and he could feel the burn on his cheek where her lips had touched him. He ached with longing for more. He switched off all the lights, grabbed a drink from the kitchen and headed for bed himself. After hanging up his suit, he pulled back the duvet and slumped into bed, one hand behind his head as he stared up at the ceiling.

It had been an interesting night with his Calendar Girl.

I wanted to kiss her.

But she's my friend.

I can't lose her as a friend.

I wouldn't be able to bear it.

But what if they gained so much more?

Sleep was a long time coming, and by the time he finally drifted off into the land of nod he'd pretty much memorised exactly how his bedroom ceiling looked in the dark.

In the next room, Callie also lay staring at the ceiling. Her stomach was comfortably full with rich food and she felt a nice warm buzz from the evening. It had been good to spend some time with Lucas away from work, away from the hospital, out on a social basis. They hadn't done that for...

God...years!

They'd had a nice night. He'd looked totally amazing too! When she'd come out of her room and seen him standing there in the middle of his flat in his dinner jacket she'd practically melted with desire. Where had this *sexy* Lucas emerged from? He could have been James Bond, he'd looked so yummy!

It's just hormones. You know it is. You tell women that every day.

Didn't make it easy, though. He'd kept taking her hand at dinner and it had been *so difficult* to remember that they were just friends and nothing else.

Her hand went beneath the covers and rested on her barely-there bump. She spoke to it, whispering soft words that meant so very much.

'I'll not hurt your daddy. I'll make sure I do right by him. Even if that means I have to walk away.'

For Callie, sleep didn't come easily either.

CHAPTER FOUR

THE NEXT FEW weeks were strange as they got used to living with each other. Waking up in the morning and finding Lucas in the next room, ready to have breakfast with her, seemed odd, but enjoyable.

She liked the way he was always there when she needed someone to talk to. She didn't have to phone him and make a time to come round, she didn't have to seek permission to be with him, and she didn't have to make an appointment—like she had to if she wanted to see her mother.

He cooked her some delicious meals, and once he even rubbed her feet after she'd had a particularly exhausting day. That had been surprising. Not the foot-rub, but the thoughts that had gone through her head as he'd done it! He had a wonderful way with his fingers. His large hands had enveloped her feet individually, their warmth caressing her tired muscles as his fingertips pressed and glided and worked out the knots. Firm where they needed to be, gentle and delicate in other places.

Her thoughts had run to how Lucas might be as a lover, though it had felt strange to allow herself even to think of him that way when he'd always been her friend. He'd had a masterful way with her feet, anyway, and she could only imagine the wonderful sensations he'd produce if his hands were let loose on the rest of her body!

And every night she'd chastely wish him good-night and go to her room feeling alone.

Odd how I feel alone even though I'm living with someone.

Callie had just turned eighteen weeks in her pregnancy, and was beginning to show much more. She went into work most days feeling tired and sleepy. Sleep had evaded her for many of her nights, and she didn't think it was because she was sleeping somewhere different. The bed in her room was comfortable, the mattress firm. She was warm enough. It was just that her head was brimming with too many thoughts...

Would she be a mother?

Wouldn't she?

Where were things heading with Lucas?

What would this do to their friendship?

She hoped it would strengthen it. After all, they'd been best friends for years and now a baby was involved...half her, half Lucas.

If I had ever changed my mind about wanting a child I'd have wanted it to be with Lucas.

That was the main thought that kept spinning round her head, rattling its way into all the corners like a whirling dervish. Not that she'd admitted to that at the fertility clinic when they'd all had to go through counselling. She knew she could never admit that.

Her thoughts were spilling over into her consciousness and making her fret and worry over lots of little things. Neither of them had come up with many answers, though she now knew that Lucas would like her to be involved as much as possible.

And that's the big question for me.

Can I be involved? And by how much?

What form would that involvement take? Neither of them

had been specific, and the idea of being a full-time mother scared her still.

I don't know if I have it in me to do that. What if I get things wrong?

Originally she'd have been on the sidelines. The baby would have been Lucas and Maggie's child and Callie would only have been involved whenever she'd visited them, or if—as Lucas had once suggested very early on— she'd became a godparent to the child.

She'd agreed to that. After all, how many godparents actually ended up having to look after a child because something tragic had happened to both its parents?

Hardly ever. In fact she knew of no circumstances in which that had happened to *anyone*. So for her it had been an easy thing to agree to. A godparent could be as close as he or she wanted.

But an actual *mother*?

I wouldn't know what to do. If I get things wrong... I have no frame of reference for what a good mother is...

And now Maggie was gone. Lucas would happily raise the child on his own. She knew in her heart that he would be more than capable of doing so. She still didn't have to be involved. She could still be a godparent.

But it's different now. If I'm to be its mother, then I want it to have the best childhood. Nothing like mine. And how could I explain to that child why I walked away?

What would Lucas think of her if she *did* walk away?

Maggie was gone and Lucas wanted Callie to be in- volved and, damn it, her hormones were affecting her more than she'd ever thought that they would! On the scan day she'd been so determined not to get attached, not to get excited at what she might see. To keep her distance just as Rhea had wanted to.

After all, hadn't she been taught how to do that by a master? It should have been easy...

But then the baby had been there, right before her eyes, on the screen. Curled up, rounded like a bean, softly nestled safe in her womb, its heart beating away, unaware of the situation its parents faced.

Totally innocent. It had no preconceptions. It was simply a baby. A baby that would be born into the world not knowing whether it would have one, two or any parents to care for it.

Callie changed from her day clothes into scrubs, attached her name tag and filled her pockets with all the paraphernalia she carried with her at work—scissors, pens, a small notepad, tape measure… She pinned her pink fob watch to her top and clipped her hand scrub to the bottom, where it was easily accessible. Then she pulled her hair up to keep it out of her face and headed to the reception area of Antenatal, where the staff hand-over at shift-change took place.

The supervisor of midwives, Sarah, was leading the hand-over and she stood in front of a busy board. All the rooms were filled with labouring mothers and Callie sensed a hectic shift.

Sarah turned to Callie. 'Callie, I'd like you in Room Six. Dr Gold will be assisting. In fact he may already be in there. Jenny Cole—she's thirty-six and a first time mother. She's diabetic and we think it's a very large baby. She's got no birth partner. There doesn't seem to be any close family.'

'Okay.'

Callie loved working with Lucas. He was just so good and efficient. Yes, all registrars were probably the same, but she *knew* Lucas and that made it different. Though she was a very capable midwife on her own, she felt safer knowing that he was in the room, backing her up. There had been so many times when he'd been there for her. And not just for her but the whole team. Calm in a crisis, efficient, direct when he needed to be, and an absolute rock in an emergency situation. Everyone knew they could rely on him and Callie had never heard anyone say a bad word about Lucas Gold.

In Room Six, Callie nodded to Lucas as she entered and then introduced herself to Jenny. Her patient appeared to be coping with her contractions well and was simply breathing her way through them.

'I'm just going to have a quick read-through of your notes.'

Callie stood at the end of the bed as Lucas checked the trace. It all seemed to be going well. According to Jenny's notes, at her last scan just two weeks ago her baby had already been estimated to be at ten pounds. Callie had a quick feel of Jenny's abdomen. Baby was head down, engaged almost four-fifths, and definitely felt extremely large.

As Jenny put in earphones to listen to soothing music Callie stepped over to Lucas. 'What's your idea for delivery?'

'I think when the time comes we'll have everyone on standby. If this baby is as big as we think it is I want to know people will be available if it becomes an emergency.'

Callie nodded. 'How come she's not having a C-section?'

'She was offered one in clinic, but she insisted on trying for a natural birth. She was adamant.'

Fair enough. Callie felt that a mother *should* try for a natural birth if that was what she wished. Though she had reservations about that if there was a risk to either mother or baby. Still, it was not her place to make a judgement. She was there to support Jenny in her wishes.

Jenny removed one of her earbuds. 'Is that a little bump I see?' She nodded at Callie's stomach.

Blushing, Callie nodded. 'Still a long way to go yet.'

'It's exciting, isn't it?'

Exciting wasn't the word... It had been a real roller-coaster since Maggie had left. Callie made a non-committal noise. It was difficult to answer with Lucas in the room. If she said it *was* exciting would he think she was thinking of being there for the baby? If she said it wasn't, then what would Jenny think?

'I've waited an age to have a baby...' Jenny breathed out happily.

'I saw in your notes you used a sperm donor?'

'Best decision I ever made. No health problems. An academic. Similar physical attributes to me. And no worries about anyone making demands to be involved. Perfect.'

'What does everyone else think of your choice?' Callie was curious.

'Mum and Dad were very supportive once they got over the shock. They wanted me to be in a relationship, you know?'

Callie nodded. Wasn't that how everyone expected it would go?

'Lots of good friends?'

'Loads. All dying to be aunts and uncles.'

Lucas came to stand by the bed. 'It's good to have a large support network. I grew up in a big family, so I can't possibly imagine what it might be like to not have anyone.'

Jenny looked at him, blushing slightly. 'Are you married, Dr Gold?'

Since becoming pregnant with his child Callie was beginning to notice the effect Lucas had on other women. It was something she'd always been aware of but hadn't really paid any attention to. But now it was different. She could see them looking at him. Sizing him up. Noting the absence of a ring on his finger. And she wasn't sure if she liked it.

He glanced at Callie. 'I'm not, no.'

'But you have a big family? That's good.'

Callie wondered what it might be like to have a supportive parent? How did that feel? To have a parent on the other end of the phone you could just talk with or pour your heart out to? What would it feel like to know you could just call round to your parents' house and *know* that you'd be welcome? That they'd make you tea, serve you biscuits, tell you the latest about so-and-so down the street?

It was so different for Callie. She couldn't imagine having that kind of relationship with her mum at all. Maria had never, *ever* been there for her on the end of a phone.

'What about you, Callie?' Jenny asked.

Callie glanced at Lucas and saw that he was staring at her with an intense look in his face. She could see he was intrigued to hear her answer, but she felt like a rabbit caught in the headlights.

What could she say? That she had an alcoholic mother, no siblings, and no idea if she was keeping the baby she was carrying? That she was considering giving away her own child? That she might have to?

How easy it had seemed months ago to agree to that. Whilst she wasn't pregnant. Whilst Maggie and Lucas were still together and married. It had been a future event—one that hadn't actually seemed real. And what maternal instincts had Callie had? None. Zero. And she'd been happy for it to be that way. Which was what she'd told everyone.

She could still enjoy babies. Other people's babies. Which was why she'd become a midwife. Callie was fascinated by pregnancy—how a woman's body nurtured and grew a baby in order to birth it and create brand-new life. A pure life, unburdened by worry, regret, selfishness or ego.

And each baby would go home with its mother and she would help another woman. And another.

Each case was different, but mostly she got to share in the joy of creating a child. Bringing a brand-new person into the world, their pages unwritten.

It was the hope she loved. That each new baby she saw would go home with its parents and have a fabulous life. The kind of life she'd never had herself.

Callie's cheeks flushed under the intensity of Lucas's gaze, the heat searing her skin as if she was being roasted on a spit over a flaming hot barbecue.

'I…there's just me, really.' She smiled and fiddled with Jenny's bed sheet, making it lie flat on the bed.

Lucas raised an eyebrow at her and she felt her heart skip a beat. She was having palpitations over Lucas as she stood at a patient's bedside!

What was happening here with Lucas? How had he gone from just being her friend to being this *man*, this *sexy, alluring guy*, since she'd conceived his child? She'd understand it if they'd slept together, or something, but they hadn't. Their baby had been conceived in a laboratory—the most unsexy, least alluring conception you could ever imagine. The most he'd done was hold her hand as the fertility specialist had positioned the fertilised egg in her womb.

Hand-holding! That was all! But now the morning sickness had passed, coupled with the fact that he was now a single man and she was carrying his baby—which was also hers as she'd used her own eggs—it was as if her body *knew* that this was the man she should have. The man she caught looking at her oddly at times…the man whose sofa she shared, whose genes she carried. Technically she should let him take her to bed and have him make her tremble and quiver with delight…

How had that happened? One minute Lucas was her best friend, a good laugh, a dependable guy—yes, he was good-looking, but she'd always believed herself immune to those good looks of his—and then the next minute, when she was knocked up with his baby, Lucas became this scintillating, sexy, so-hot-he-looked-airbrushed kind of guy, whom she lived with, slept in the next room to…a please-can-I-get-into-your-bed kind of guy.

It was madness. Madness!

Dragging her eyes away from Lucas's steely blues, she blushed once again and smiled at Jenny.

'I'm going to be the best mum this little girl could ever have,' Jenny said.

'I'm sure of it,' Callie said. Though part of her wondered how she could be so sure for someone else but couldn't apply that certainty to herself.

Jenny delivered her baby girl some hours later. Ten pounds exactly. She gave birth beautifully and it was a very smooth delivery, even though there'd been a fear that there might be a shoulder dystocia when the baby's shoulders had got stuck in the birth canal. But everything had gone well.

Only when Jenny and her daughter, Camille, were settled on a postnatal ward, with the baby feeding well, did Callie go for a sit-down in the staffroom.

She was tired…exhausted. It would be so easy to close her eyes. But as she sat there with her feet up she felt a little something swirling around in her stomach. She laid a hand on her round abdomen.

Was the baby kicking?

She must have had the strangest look on her face, for when Lucas came into the staffroom to grab a coffee and saw her frozen, waiting for something to happen again, he asked, 'You okay?'

'I felt something.'

'Pain?' Fear was etched into his features.

'No, not pain…'

'Is the baby moving?' A beam of a smile broke out across his face and he shot across the room to join her.

'I don't know…' She moved her hand to feel again.

'Is it doing it now?'

He reached out and laid a hand on her stomach—the first time he'd done so. She could feel the heat of his hand through her scrubs and found herself hoping the baby would make one of its swishing movements.

It did.

'Oh, my God!' He pulled his hand away, his face lit up with delight. 'I felt that!'

So had she. And though she was delighted the baby had moved for him she found herself wishing he'd lay his hands on her again.

Oh, my goodness, these pregnancy hormones!

She flushed and had to use a piece of card to wave at her face and cool herself down.

'Are you all right?'

'Absolutely. Just a little hot flush.'

Putting her feet up, she lay back on the chair and ran her hands over her growing baby bump. She was quite happy with her bump. Pleased that as yet she had no stretch marks.

Inside, her baby gave her another little swirl and she gasped out loud as she felt it through her skin. She wanted to see if she could *see* the baby move, and raised her scrubs over the bump to reveal her bare belly.

This time there were no scrubs between them. This time Lucas had his hands on her bare abdomen, cupping the small mound of her growing uterus as the baby flipped and swished and generally swam about inside.

'That's amazing!'

'It knows you're its daddy.'

'Maybe.' He nestled closer to her and laid his head against her stomach. She could feel the bristles from his jaw prickling her skin. 'I can't hear it.'

'Give it a few months.'

He looked up at her, one hand still on her abdomen. 'I'm glad I'm having the baby with you.'

Callie looked back at him, shocked at his words. For weeks they'd danced around the subject, since that night at Gianni's, but now he was getting all serious again. 'Are you?'

'Yes. I couldn't have wished for it to be with anyone else.'

She gulped, her face flushing with heat and tension. 'Really?'

'You're my best friend.'

'I'm not very maternal.'

He looked deep into her eyes. 'You are. Or you wouldn't worry so much about doing the right thing.'

'You know I worry?'

'Of course. I worry too. We didn't get ourselves into this situation in the conventional way, did we?'

'I guess not.'

'I don't want that to matter anymore.'

She sat there, tummy exposed, his hand still resting on it just above the belly button, aware of his touch, aware of his nearness, and aware that his lips looked ever so kissable!

He got up off the floor and sat on the sofa next to her. He was close. Unbearably so.

Her heart began to pound as her breath caught in her throat. Her skin had come alive at his touch, tingling and yearning for more.

He's going to kiss me!

And she realised she wanted him to. Wanted it more than anything else in the whole wide world!

She sat up slightly and met him halfway, wrapping her hand behind his neck, embedding her fingers in his tousled hair and pulling his face towards hers, meeting his lips with hers, indulging in a wonderful, tentative, exploring first kiss.

Fireworks were going off throughout her body. She felt tense and relaxed and excited all at once. Her hands itched for his touch, to be holding him. Their mouths opened as the kiss deepened and his tongue took hers, and then she was breathing him, kissing him, holding him, in a way she'd never felt with a man before. His bristles scorched her face and it was a sweet agony as passion took them both by surprise and hunger for each other burned them to their very core.

This is Lucas!

Of course it was! He'd been there in front of her all this time, the man for her, and she'd let him be just a friend for all that time—not knowing, never allowing herself to think about it. *Why* hadn't she thought about it?

Perhaps I did. In fact, I know I did!

She'd once let the thought of what it would be like to sleep with Lucas occupy her mind for many a night.

But she'd not wanted to risk their friendship. She'd not allowed herself to linger on the prospect. She'd always dismissed it. It had been wrong before—he'd been with someone else, and she'd been his friend.

I need to breathe.

She couldn't remember how. Instead she continued to kiss him, to feel his soft hair in her fingers, his chest against hers, the yearning for more… She moaned softly and it seemed to increase his ardour. He mumbled her name.

For so long she'd wondered what it would be like. This moment. This kiss. Yet never in her wildest dreams had she thought she'd be thinking about ending it.

She knew she had to stop it. Knew she had to let him go. Because this wasn't meant to happen! If she lost him as a friend they would endanger everything they'd held dear about their friendship. And if she let things continue in this vein and it didn't work out… Well, where would they be then? Parents living in separate houses, meeting in rooms where the tension would be so thick it would need to be chopped with an axe, not sliced with a knife.

She knew that was what happened. She'd experienced that when her mother had broken up with her many boyfriends. When Lucas had broken up with girls in school and he'd confided in her about how awkward a particular class had been.

It never went well. People would *say* they'd remain friends, but that never happened in her experience. They separated. Pretended for a while and then drifted apart. Far apart.

She could never allow that to happen with Lucas.

Callie pulled back and stared into his eyes. Absently, she touched her swollen lips with her fingertips and then she stood up quickly, putting physical distance between them as she pulled her scrubs back over her stomach and put her hands solidly into her pockets.

'We shouldn't do that.' She sounded breathless. 'We can't risk it… There's a baby now—we have to think about that.'

Lucas looked hurt, but then the shutters came down. 'Sure.' He licked his lips. 'Not a problem. I'd better get back to work.'

She watched him go, her heart breaking, wishing she could take back her words but knowing that she couldn't. But he must have thought the same thing as her. Why else would he have backed off so easily?

We have to be sensible about this. We can't risk what we have…

The baby began to swish again with all the excitement. Callie laid her hand on her stomach. 'I can do this,' she said.

Callie wished she could be sure of that. She was certain Lucas would make a good dad—she believed in him. Knew he would be.

It was her own maternal instincts she doubted.

Lucas stood in Theatre, suturing a wound, his face a mask of concentration. Anyone on the outside looking in would think that he was simply concentrating on the task at hand—and he was. It was just that he was also thinking about what had happened with Callie.

She let me kiss her!

She'd more than *let* him. She'd *welcomed* it! Hadn't she? At first? Just after the baby had started kicking and he'd been touching her belly?

His hands had felt alive at the softness of her skin and the roundness of her belly, each nerve-ending dancing with excitement. Not just from feeling the baby move, but from touching *her.*

When had he ever touched her so intimately?

Never.

Callie didn't invite touching. Never had. He'd always known to keep his distance in that way. But with the baby moving...

They'd been able to share a wonderful, cherished, delightful moment—each of them feeling the child they had created together. But it had also been the first time he'd ever properly laid his hands on her.

The way she'd looked at him! He would swear blind she'd had something akin to desire in her eyes! Her pupils had widened, her breath had hitched in her throat and he'd sensed her pulse beating rapidly... It had been too magical a moment *not* to kiss her.

And what a kiss!

He'd never felt that way from just a kiss before. It had been like waking up from a deep sleep and realising that after all this time, all the years with Maggie, the kisses meant nothing compared to this one. With Callie it had been so special, so tender—as if his lips had discovered what they were truly meant to do. They were meant to be connected to Callie. They were for her and her alone.

His whole body had come alive. Each nerve-ending tingling, every synapse in his brain firing away like a space rocket. His heart had pounded and adrenaline had rushed through him, awakening every muscle, every intention, daring him to touch her more, to wrap his arms around her and pull her close, to envelop her as much as he could.

Fighting that had been difficult. Because there'd been fear there, too. Fear that she would stop him. Fear that she would break away. And if she did what would she say? What would she do? She was so afraid of losing their friendship and he...he was afraid she'd push him away. She'd already done it once, broken his heart once, why wouldn't she do it again?

And she had.

She'd stopped the kiss, shut them both down, before he could get carried away.

Perhaps that had been wise? Perhaps it was good that she'd put the brakes on? After all, he had no real idea of what she actually *felt*. Hadn't he already rushed into one relationship? Look how that had turned out! Wouldn't he be foolish to do the same thing with Callie? The one person who mattered the most to him.

The suturing done, he snipped the stitch and pulled down his mask. 'I'm done.'

The theatre assistants nodded and watched him walk away.

But as he stood at the sink, firmly scrubbing his arms with iodine soap, he knew—just knew in his heart—that this time, no matter what, he would treat Callie better than he had his wife.

The kiss—though heart-poundingly amazing—had been wrong. Callie had been right to stop it. They could never be together in that way and no matter what he felt for her he had to get over it—or he knew he'd get hurt again.

CHAPTER FIVE

OVER THE NEXT couple of weeks Callie realised that the baby's movements were going from being 'swishy' to definite kicks. Their baby liked moving. *A lot*. She knew she had to keep track of the movements and make sure she felt ten or more each day—and as the days passed she had no problem surpassing that total.

She had a very active baby, and she enjoyed nothing more than lying in the bath and watching the somersaults going on inside, as her belly wobbled from one side to the other, or was poked up in one area as the baby stretched its legs. There were times when a foot would press up against her belly and she could push it back down with her finger. Other times the foot would keep pressing out, as if the baby were playing with her.

Every evening they were at home together Lucas would sit with her, his hand on her belly, and talk to the baby. They were moments that she treasured, not knowing for how much longer this closeness might last, so she eked out every last second of the time.

They jokingly referred to the baby as 'Bean', and there was nothing she enjoyed more than to have Lucas tell the baby a story. He'd once read *Jack and the Beanstalk* to it, and every time he'd got to the *fee-fie-fo-fum* the baby had kicked madly and wriggled, making them laugh with delight and joy.

They both thought they were having a boy, but the discussion came up as to whether they ought to find out at the next day's twenty-week scan.

'It might be nice to know for sure,' Callie said. Then she'd know what she'd be giving away. A son? A daughter?

'I don't know. I kind of like the surprise.'

'Well, it's going to be one or the other, isn't it? If you find out what sex it is then you can start thinking about names and how you might want to decorate the nursery.'

The nursery was going to be the room that Callie was currently staying in. It was currently a pale blue, but they both knew that babies preferred strong colours to pale ones, so it would need redecorating.

'Don't you want to know if you're having a son or a daughter?'

'I'll be overjoyed either way.' He shrugged. It was a simple matter for him, it seemed. 'And *we* will pick names and *we* will think about how *we* want to decorate the nursery. I don't want to hear any more of this "you" stuff.'

'But it's *your* baby, Lucas. I was never meant to be involved.'

He shook his head defiantly. 'But you *are*. Things are different now and I want your input.'

How could she explain? If she got involved—if she started making choices—then she might get too attached. What would happen then if it all went pear-shaped? If it all went wrong? She couldn't bear to lose him.

'I'm not sure that I should give it.'

He looked at her sideways. 'Why are you afraid, Callie?'

'I don't know! Because I'm not sure how good I'm going to be for the baby. What role model did I have? A lying drunk who couldn't even be bothered to think of a proper name for me. A sly, selfish monster who loved alcohol more than she did finding food for our table. I don't know how to connect with a child—'

'Ridiculous! So Maria was an awful mother? You think that will make *you* a bad one too? You see women at work every day from all social backgrounds, having been through neglect and abuse and poverty, and they prove that they can be the best mothers *because* they had such an awful time themselves. Look at how Jenny was. She didn't even have parents, and yet she knew she was going to be the best parent she could for her little girl. You can do that too.'

'I know. I know you're right. But I still worry. I never thought that I'd have a child, and now that I am I need to know that I'm doing the right thing for it.'

'If you really were such a cold fish—if I thought in any way, shape or form that you were a cold-hearted, selfish monster—do you think we would have stayed friends as long as we have? You're *lovely*, Callie. You're kind, and you have the biggest heart of anyone I know.'

He was looking into her eyes so intently it was difficult to stop the somersaults in her tummy. Ever since they'd kissed that time his close proximity, his intensity when he looked at her, sparked her awareness of him. The way he moved, his scent, the way he gazed at her when he thought she wasn't looking... She knew there was the possibility of something else developing between them. And that scared her too.

'Really?'

'Do selfish people offer to have babies for someone else?'

She could see his point. But she'd never told him that she'd once entertained the idea that they *could* get together. That she'd thought if she was ever going to have a baby with anyone she would have chosen him. She'd not told the clinic. Had deliberately lied to them all. Because when he'd asked her out it had been the toughest thing for her to turn him down. Because she'd known she had to do something she didn't want to do. To the one man she'd wanted to say yes to!

But she'd not wanted to lose him as a friend if anything had gone wrong. All his relationships with women up until that point had been short ones. They'd all started with passion and *'Isn't she amazing?'* and then they'd all ended.

Callie couldn't have borne to be one of those girls.

Couldn't have borne to lose the one rock who had always been there for her through her childhood. Her one shoulder to cry on. The one person who would actually listen to her. Comfort her. Hold her.

Did he know that he was the only person who had ever held her? Properly? Just to enjoy holding her and not want something else?

It had been a big thing for her to offer to be his surrogate—especially when she'd known she'd be using her own eggs…that the baby she'd be giving away would be biologically half hers.

'Talking of Maria—she rang this morning and left a message. I think you ought to go and see her. She clearly wants to make amends.'

Callie visibly sagged. 'I can't bear to be let down again, Lucas.'

He touched her hand and she squeezed his fingers in response. 'But if she really has turned a corner—if she really has been off the booze for six months—you could have that relationship with her you've always wanted.'

He was looking at her strangely again. Was he thinking about *them*? About the relationship that he'd once wanted?

But he was right. Her craving for a relationship with her mother had been long buried, but it was still there. If there was any chance at all that Maria had turned a corner…

'Would you come with me?'

'Of course I will.'

There was an intensity in their stares as their gazes locked, and suddenly Callie was aware of how close Lucas was. It would be so easy to lean forward and kiss him again, to allow themselves to lose each other in the moment again, but she knew she couldn't let that happen.

She pulled her hand free and stood up. 'Cup of tea?'

He looked disappointed at her putting distance between them, but then his face went serious, and she hoped he realised she was doing a good thing by keeping her distance.

We can't be together like that, no matter how much we want it. But, damn, it's so hard to get to sleep at night, knowing he's just next door...

By the next morning, the day of the scan—a day off for both of them—they still hadn't reached a decision. They sat in the same chairs they'd sat in at the first scan, waiting nervously.

'Can you remember the last time we sat here?' Lucas asked.

She nodded, watching a mother opposite them try to play with her toddler, who'd found a set of bricks and was stacking them rather unsuccessfully. 'Seems such a long time ago. So much has changed since then.'

He reached over to grab her hand. 'Good changes?'

She smiled back and squeezed his fingers. 'Definitely. But if you'd told me weeks ago that it would end up like this...I would never have believed you.'

He smiled. 'But I'm happy it has. Aren't you?'

Callie shrugged, noncommittal. 'Just...you know...at the beginning the set-up was different, wasn't it? I went into this pregnancy knowing I was going to give away the baby, and then everything got thrown up into the air. That was what I meant.'

'So *are* we finding out? The sex?' he asked. 'I'll let you choose.'

It was a nice gesture. But she knew he didn't want to

know and so decided to side with him. 'We'll leave it as a surprise.'

'Okay.'

They waited another ten minutes or so before they got called through, during which time the toddler tottered over, grinning and dribbling, grabbing on to Lucas's legs for stability.

'Hey, hello there.' He smiled at the little boy and Callie loved watching them interact.

He's so good with him! Lucas is going to be a great dad! But how does he make it look so easy?

She was glad the toddler hadn't come to *her*. She'd have felt awkward and the toddler probably would have cried—she knew it. She still wasn't sure what type of mother she'd make as she had no frame of reference as to what a good mother was.

Lucas had told her once that she didn't need a frame of reference. That she could learn as she went and that, seeing as Callie wasn't an alcoholic or anything like her own mother, the likelihood of her being a good mother was strong.

'Being a parent doesn't come with an instruction guide, Callie. People learn as they go. You think no one else is afraid?' he'd asked her once. He'd really got angry. Frustrated that she just wouldn't agree to the possibility that she might be a good mother.

She hoped beyond hope that he was right.

Eventually, her name was called and they went in. It was Sophie again.

'Hi, guys, nice to see you again. You're looking well, Callie. Blooming.'

Callie smiled and heaved herself onto the bed. 'Bigger this time.'

'Definitely. You've been okay? Everything normal?'

'Oh, yes.'

'Baby moving lots?'

'Like a trapeze artist.'

Sophie grinned. 'That's what we like to hear. Okay, same procedure as before. Lie back, I'll put the gel on and then we'll have a look around. It'll be a longer scan this time, because we use this one to check for any anomalies or soft markers that might indicate a problem.'

'Sure—I know.'

'Of course. I'm so used to explaining everything I forget this is probably old hat to you.'

'Not really. It's all quite scary when it's your own.' She reached out for Lucas's reassuring hand, surprising herself. Where had 'hands-off' Callie gone?

Sophie nodded and tucked paper towel into the top of Callie's underwear.

'Right…we'll have a general look round first, then I'll take four measurements today. The biparietal diameter to measure the baby's head, the abdominal circumference, head circumference and femur length. We'll check that against gestation and decide which percentile your baby is in. Do you want to know the sex today?' They looked at each other to confirm what they'd decided earlier. Lucas gave her a nod. Callie turned back to Sophie. 'No, we don't. We want a surprise.'

'Excellent. Okay. And so we begin…'

As before, Sophie kept the screen to herself until she'd found the heartbeat and could see the baby moving, and then she turned the screen so that both of them could see.

Callie gasped aloud. 'Wow! It's so big this time!'

'Baby's grown beautifully,' Sophie agreed.

Lucas squeezed her hand. But Callie couldn't take her eyes off the screen. There was their baby! Their beautiful baby! Moving and tumbling and sucking its thumb. It was all so clear! A real person. A new human being. *Theirs*.

Sophie was clicking and moving the mouse around, looking at the head, the brain.

'Beautiful butterfly patterning—just what we'd expect to see.'

Then she went down through the baby's body, checking various organs and pointing them out: the kidneys, the heart. Even their baby's bladder, which had some urine in it, was sweet to see! She checked legs and feet, then arms and hands, and then she turned to the blacker parts of the scan.

'I'm just going to measure the amniotic fluid around baby first.' She moved a small white cross from one side of the expanse of black across to the other and clicked again. Then she moved the transducer and took another measurement. 'Fluid's good.' As she worked she kept clicking to print the pictures. 'No soft markers that I can see. I'll do the measurements now.'

Callie gazed on in awe.

You're my baby. Our baby. The last time I saw you I had no idea if you'd be mine. Now... Well, now I'm allowing myself to think that you might be.

The thought didn't surprise her. Which *did* surprise her. It seemed natural to want this baby.

'So, how far along are you now, Callie?'

'Twenty weeks and six days.'

'Okay. That's good. I can use that against the measurements in a minute. I just need to check where the placenta is lying.'

Callie knew this was very important. Not that the other measurements weren't important too, but if there was a problem with the position of the placenta it might jeopardise her chances of a normal delivery. If, for example, the placenta was low down and covering the cervix, the baby would not be able to come out of the birth canal. What they needed to hear now was that the placenta was posterior, or placed high.

'It's just slightly covering the cervix, but you've got time for it to move up, out of the way. We'll keep an eye on it. Arrange for another scan.'

Callie let out a breath she hadn't known she'd been holding. 'Right.'

They both watched intently as Sophie carefully skirted around the pelvic area of the baby—without giving the game away—and took abdominal and femur measurements. Then she did the head, taking the two measurements she needed to check for proper growth.

Sophie wrote everything down in Callie's notes and then plotted the measurements onto a graph. She showed the results to them. 'Everything's perfect. Baby's on the seventy-fifth percentile for all of these, so he or she is growing properly in all the right places, and for the right gestation.'

'Good.' Callie took the long stream of photos that Sophie had printed off for them. 'Thanks.'

'Do you want a 3D picture of baby's face?'

They looked at each other. Then Callie turned back to Sophie. 'Yes, please.'

Sophie pressed a button to change the scan picture from two-dimensional to three. The grainy black and white disappeared and was replaced by a sepia-type colour as Sophie brought the transducer up to their baby's face. Part of it was obscured by a hand and the umbilical cord, but most of it could be seen.

'Oh, my God!'

Sophie clicked and a picture slid out of the machine.

Callie held it so Lucas could also see. He couldn't stop grinning.

He leaned down and kissed Callie on the cheek. 'Beautiful—like you.'

She flushed at the compliment—and at the burn of his lips on her skin.

Sophie smiled. 'Everything's normal. Progressing as it should be. Now, do you have any questions?'

They didn't.

'Can't think of any.'

'Okay. So we'll arrange for another scan in a few weeks—just to check the placenta has moved off the cervix. But if you have a bleed you must come straight in. Although at the moment I couldn't see any reason why that might happen.'

'You have to warn us just in case. Don't worry—we understand.'

Sophie nodded. 'Okay. Have a nice day, you two.' She stood and opened the door once Callie was cleaned of gel and covered up again.

They walked out into the light of the waiting area and hugged each other. The moment had been perfect.

'Do you think *she* knows?' Lucas asked.

'Knows what?'

'The sex of the baby.'

'Probably.'

'Hmm, I thought so too. Seems kind of odd that she knows and we don't.'

Callie looked at him thoughtfully. 'Do you want to go back and ask? I won't mind.'

Briefly it tempted him, but then he shook his head. 'No. We agreed on a surprise and a surprise we'll get. Let's get home and have something to eat. I'm starving.'

'I thought we could go over to Laurie Park. The weather's nice—we could go out on the boating lake.'

'Sounds good.'

Lucas drove them home and they packed a picnic for Laurie Park. It was a beautiful place, filled with fruit trees and harvest bushes. It was a 'free food forest'—following an idea that had started in Seattle, America, and travelled across the pond. It had been specifically created and designed to be filled with fruit-providing trees and shrubs and plants, so that people could pick and harvest for free. Callie thought it was an ingenious idea, but hadn't been there yet.

In the centre of the park there was a boating lake, with an island at its centre established as a nature reserve, where you had to keep to certain paths and picnic areas. This was where they headed.

The weather was beautiful and sunny, and Callie couldn't help but admire Lucas's muscles as he rowed the boat. His short-sleeved shirt showed off his tanned skin and muscular arms to perfection and it was nice to see him relaxed—not the intense Lucas she usually saw at work, with a stethoscope draped around his neck.

They moored the small rowing boat at one of the wooden jetties and Lucas got off first, then reached down to help her out so she didn't slip or fall. She tried not to pay too much attention to how she felt whilst he held her hand, deliberately ignoring the wish that he would continue to hold it.

The boat wobbled as she stood, scaring her for a moment, but Lucas kept hold of her firmly until she was off. He took the picnic basket in one hand and walked beside her as she delighted in the different berries and fruits she saw, picking some for their meal.

The sun was hot and it was the type of weather in which you might easily burn. She was glad she'd chosen her summer dress. The dress was the first bit of maternity clothing she'd ever bought, knowing she would be carrying her baby through the long, hot summer months.

There weren't many people about on the small island, and no one else in the picnic area they chose. They spread a tartan blanket on the ground and began to lay out their food.

'It's beautiful here.' Callie remarked, looking out over the fresh green grass and through the woodland glade to the calm water of the lake. There were swans gliding smoothly over the surface, two grey cygnets behind them.

'It certainly is. You'd never imagine we were in London.'

'No.'

He reached out to smooth a tendril of hair away from her face and she awkwardly tucked it behind her ear, flushing slightly at the intimate touch. What was he doing? Didn't he know he shouldn't touch her like that? They'd kissed once, but that had been a mistake. It couldn't happen again. They were just friends.

Callie finished laying out the picnic: baguettes, cheese, fruit, fruit juices, deli meats and strawberry jelly—her current craving. Lucas laughed when he saw she'd brought it.

'I couldn't come out without it.'

'Our baby is going to have a sweet tooth.'

'Oh, I don't know…my mum drank all that alcohol and I'm not an alcoholic.'

She knew she shouldn't have said it. It had put a dampener on things as soon as it was out of her mouth.

'Sorry. Forget what I said.'

'We can talk about it if you want?'

She shrugged. 'I was being flippant.'

'But it's important to you. It's part of your history.'

She poured out some fruit juice. 'Okay…where do I start?' She shielded her eyes from the sun, wishing she'd brought sunglasses. 'Well, I guess I was lucky I didn't have foetal alcohol syndrome when I was born. I was small—only about four pounds, though I was full term—and they reckoned I had a small heart murmur, but that was it. The murmur's gone now, thankfully, but I was so worried about today's scan.'

'Even though you don't drink?'

'Even though I don't drink. I was worried that because I got away with it as a child there might be a problem with *your* baby instead. Jump a generation—that sort of thing.'

He smiled. '*Our* baby.'

'Yes.' She nodded quickly, feeling awkward.

'But you know that's unfounded?'

'I know, but I can't help myself worrying.'

Lucas wafted a fly from his leg. 'You never raised this at the clinic.'

'I did. I told my counsellor when we had one-to-one sessions.'

'And what did she say?'

'Same as you. That it doesn't work that way, and that, besides, when they choose the egg and the sperm in the dish they pick the healthiest, best-developed ones. The chances of us having a problem was going to be minimal. And they'd done the genetic testing, too. I'm just an old worrywart.'

He leaned forward. 'It's because you care. You're going to be a great mum, Callie, because *you* have that quality. Your mum didn't for a reason. Her alcoholism is a disease which you don't have. Please don't worry about what sort of mum *you'll* make. I *know* you'll be fine.'

It was sweet of him to say it, but he was her friend—of course he'd say that. There was still that deep-down worry that she would be an awful mother. Like Maria had been. It didn't matter that she wanted to make amends. She'd still got it badly wrong to start with.

'We'd better eat before the wasps beat us to it.' She laughed, but the laughter tailed away when she saw the stern look on his face.

'Why do you always change the subject, Callie?'

'I'm not sure I know what you mean.'

'Your being a mother. I give you a compliment, tell you you'll be fine, and you change the subject. Or you argue with me. Tell me I'm wrong.'

She shrugged. 'I was taught avoidance by a master at the craft.'

'For someone who's so afraid to be like her mother, you frequently admit her influence on you, happily accepting it.' He sounded annoyed.

'I'm not happy to accept it, Lucas. It's just the way my life was. You wouldn't understand.'

'Wouldn't I? You weren't the only one with a difficult childhood.'

She looked at him askance. 'I don't remember *you* having an alcoholic mother.'

'Don't be pedantic, Callie. I meant my father. I hardly ever saw him, and as a boy I craved that connection. When he did come home he would be angry and resentful, and smack me more times than I could count just to "make me into a man". He hated the fact that I was surrounded by nothing but women, and knew how to sew and cook rather than fish or hunt. Even my best friend was a girl, and my father hated that too. He couldn't understand why I wasn't this football and rugby-playing army cadet, ready to follow in his footsteps. Instead he'd come home from Malaysia or Singapore and find me cooped up in the kitchen with my mother and sisters, covered in flour and other baking ingredients.'

Callie looked upset. 'I'm sorry. I didn't mean to be flippant.'

'I'm just saying you weren't the only one with a bad childhood.' He sighed. 'I craved my father's approval and attention just as much as you craved your mother's. Neither of us got what we wanted.' He looked at her as the wind billowed her hair around her face. 'Or *who* we wanted.'

There was an awkward silence filled only by birdsong and the gentle humming of nearby bees.

Lucas got up and walked to the water's edge, his hands in his pockets.

Callie looked at his back as he stood by the water. So alone and remote. She felt bad, and knew she ought to go to him and apologise. This was supposed to be a nice day out for both of them. A day off from work. A day off from pressure. Time to give them both the opportunity to talk about what would soon happen.

And I've messed it up.

Callie got up from the blanket and went over to where he stood. There were some ducks happily paddling, and further along a moorhen. She reached out to touch his arm and slid her hand into his.

'I'm sorry.'

When he turned she could see the anguish on his face.

'I am too. I didn't think anything could spoil today.'

She was going to make a comment about being taught how to do that, too, then realised that it was just the sort of thing Lucas had been referring to.

'We need to talk, Lucas. Properly. About everything. The baby, the surrogacy… Everything.'

'The future?'

She nodded, blinking in the bright sun. 'Yes.'

He looked her straight in the eye. 'I want you involved, Callie. I want you to be there for our baby. I know you can be. I know you're capable. I just want you to persuade *yourself* that you can do it just as much as I know that you can.'

She wanted to believe him. She really did. But years of doubt and second-guessing everything she'd ever known was a hard habit to break. 'When you say "involved", what does that mean? Occasional visits? Being a godparent?'

'Being a *mother*.'

There. He'd said it. Out loud. Asked for a huge commitment from her. A commitment she'd not expected when she'd first gone into this surrogacy.

'But what if—?'

He grabbed her arms. 'No "what ifs", Callie! Okay, you were only going to be the surrogate to start with, but that's all changed now. We're in this together and we're best friends. I don't see why we can't do this!'

She looked deep into his eyes, aware of how firmly he was holding her, aware of the proximity of his broad chest, those strong arms that had rowed them across the lake, the healthy brown glow of his sun-drenched skin. How could she tell him she was so afraid? Afraid that she'd lose him as her friend if they took their friendship to the next level and it didn't work out.

She knew she'd just die if she didn't have him in her life, and if he stayed just a friend then she could keep him there. Anything more than that would put them at risk.

She shifted her gaze and focused on his lips. His beautiful mouth, his strong jaw. He was gazing hungrily at her, like a man who couldn't bear not to touch, and before she knew what was happening he'd pulled her against his chest and pressed his lips to hers.

She sank into his embrace, tasting him, submitting to him, sinking against his body and feeling his arousal as they kissed.

Why have we been fighting this?

It felt so natural. It felt so *good!*

Kissing Lucas felt so damn *right*, and her hands went into his hair, clutching him to her as their mouths opened, deepening the kiss, their tongues entwining. A fiery heat spread up her body, electrifying her skin with his every tender touch.

The sun beat down upon them as their own fires burned within them.

She could barely breathe. She didn't want to stop kissing him just to breathe but she had to, and as she pulled away she saw the dazed look in his eyes and knew he'd been just as physically affected by the kiss as she had.

'Lucas, we—'

He shook his head and kissed her again. More tenderly

this time, cupping her face, sliding his hands down her neck, over her shoulders, down her arms, until he pulled her firmly against his arousal once more.

Callie groaned his name as his tongue wrapped around hers searing his touch into her memory banks for evermore.

Oh, God, why can't I have him like this?

She felt dizzy. Hot. Swept away on a tide of passion that she'd never felt before. The heat deep within her began to burn, awakening after many years of being kept hidden, trapped inside, bursting forth to scream its very nature to the world.

Everything around them was forgotten. The lovely island, the beautiful warm sunshine, the romanticism of the lake. All there was—was his kiss.

Her need for Lucas was frightening, overwhelming, and suddenly she felt scared by what they were doing. She pulled free and stepped back, breaking their contact.

'Callie—'

'We should stop.' Her hands hung limply at her sides, her hair was ruffled by his hands, and the memory of his touch was burning a trace across her heart.

He looked at her, hungry for more. 'Why?'

She couldn't answer him. Why *was* she stopping them?

Because you're my friend, Lucas, and I dare not lose you if this goes wrong! I couldn't bear to be without you.

'I need time to think.' She saw the disappointment in his face, so she reached out for his hand and took it in hers. 'I'm not running away. I just…need time to absorb this.'

He nodded, reluctantly, and they went back to the blanket together. They sat and nibbled at their lunch, no longer hungry for food, looking over the water, talking about nothing. But the atmosphere was strained by what was not being said.

A mallard glided by followed by six young ducklings, all brown and yellow and chirping. Squirrels jumped from tree to tree above them, and all around was birdsong and sunshine and warmth and bees flitting from flower to flower.

It should have been perfect. It should have been easy.

She'd ruined it and hurt him again.

Eventually Lucas broke the silence. His face was grim. 'If your heart isn't in this, Callie, then I'd rather you stepped back.'

'What?' She wasn't sure she'd heard him correctly. What did he mean, 'step back'?

'If you can't commit to this one hundred per cent, then I'd rather you didn't commit at all.'

'Lucas—'

'I mean it.'

He stared at her. His eyes were telling her he would not budge on this. He would not make allowances for her. She had to decide. She had to let him know what her plans were.

A cooler breeze came along and Callie felt cold. She'd not brought a jacket or cardigan and neither had Lucas.

'We ought to head back,' he said.

'I'll gather together the picnic things,' she mumbled, but he blocked her with his arm and said he would do it.

She watched him tidy away. He was so good. He'd been so patient with her. She knew he wanted more for them and that she was unable to give it. Or too scared to give it. But she hoped that in time he would understand. Surely he valued their friendship as much as she did?

'I'm glad we came here today,' she said, trying to brighten the mood.

He nodded. 'Me too.'

'Perhaps another day we could go to Windsor Castle? I always wanted to go there, but my mother never took me.'

He sat back on his haunches, blinking in the sunlight. 'I remember. She always let you down, didn't she?'

He wasn't just talking about the castle, though, was he?

He was letting her know that he understood. About how hard it was for her.

'I'll definitely take you.'

Their eyes met and she wondered if he was still talking about taking her to the castle or *something else*? Feeling all hot and bothered suddenly, she smiled and helped him pack away the last of the things.

It would be nice to go to Windsor Castle one day.

Perhaps they'd make it?

As friends, if nothing else.

Back at the flat, Callie unpacked the picnic, put the things they hadn't used into the fridge, then headed into her room for a cardigan. As she stood by her wardrobe, deciding which one to choose, she became aware of Lucas filling the doorway.

'You okay?'

He was looking at her strangely. His beautiful blue eyes all intense and serious and dark.

'I need to tell you something, Callie. Something I wanted to say at the park, but…'

Callie closed her wardrobe and threw on the cardigan, then sat down on her bed, rubbing her abdomen as the baby kicked. 'What is it?'

He came in and knelt down in front of her, looking up into her face. 'I'm getting strong feelings for you, Callie. Feelings I never thought I'd feel again. And I want us to be honest with each other at all times.'

She nodded slowly, afraid of what he might say. He'd said 'again', reminding her of the first time he'd asked her out and she'd turned him down. But she'd been so young! As had he. It had been too scary to take that step with him then and it was even more so now! So much was at stake— not just their friendship, but the baby. Their innocent baby.

'You can be honest with me.'

'I think you ought to go and see your mother. Get some closure. See if she really has turned a corner.'

She sighed. 'I'm not sure I can cope with any more of her lies, Lucas.'

'I know. But if she's *not* lying, Callie…if she really has been on the wagon for six months and this new man has made a difference in her life…you'd be a fool to let that relationship go.' His voice softened. 'She's your *mother*. And that's a bond that can never be broken. Besides…people can change.'

He let her go and went back into the lounge, leaving her thinking over his words.

He might be right. If Maria *had* been dry for months, then didn't she owe it to her to give her another chance? Even after all her lies? After all the let-downs? If she turned away now, when there was the chance of reconciliation…

But what if Lucas was wrong? If she was still lying…?

Then I won't have lost anything. It'll just be the same as before, won't it?

But she knew he'd also been referring to her. Saying that *she* could change. That she could be the mother he believed she could be.

CHAPTER SIX

THE BANANA TASTED odd in her mouth, and after a brave attempt to finish it she pushed it away, half eaten. Life was beginning to bother her. Thoughts were keeping her awake. Feelings and physical pangs kept her hungry in more ways than one.

Lucas had said she needed closure with regard to her mother. Well, maybe she needed closure in other ways too.

When Lucas came in from work he was exhausted and needed a shower. She found herself twiddling her thumbs, then cleaning out a cupboard and reorganising a bookshelf before he emerged, hair wet, a towel around his neck and another at his waist, his bare chest and legs pebbled with moisture.

What are you doing to me?

He looked delicious. Delectable.

Edible, even.

Licking her lips, she tried to calm her twitchy fingers and the pang in her stomach that cried out for some physical contact from him. Perhaps another kiss like that one at the park, by the lake?

That had been a toe-curler in all the right places!

He had a nice flat stomach—nothing too ripped, but not flabby either. And from his belly button there was a smattering of dark hair leading down to...

To distract herself, she tried to think of Maria. Memories of her were usually perfect for dampening her mood. She spotted her favourite teddy bear, lying at an awkward angle on the table, and she reached for it to straighten it, remembering another teddy bear she'd once made.

As a child, when she'd outgrown a nightdress, rather than throw it out she'd cut it up into squares and circles and hand-sewn it into a teddy-type thing. It hadn't been pretty, or neat, but it had been girly and pink and she'd stuffed it with filling from her pillow, hoping her mum wouldn't notice the crudely cut hole in the pillow covering.

Of course her mum hadn't noticed.

Callie hadn't named it, but she had cuddled it. And for a long time she'd thought she'd known what it was to cuddle.

Until Lucas had held her.

Stop it, Callie!

Then the importance of being held by someone who loved you had suddenly became important, and she'd realised just how much she'd missed as a child.

'I'm glad you're home.'

He looked at her face and frowned. 'Sorry. I got called away. You got my note?'

'Yes. Thank you.'

She stared at him, wondering how to start, but with him dressed like that he was too much of a temptation and she took a step back.

He raised his eyebrow, then grabbed the towel around his neck and began to ruffle his dark hair.

'We've never really discussed Maggie properly, have we? When she left, I mean?'

That was it. Best to come straight out with it. Not beat around the bush.

'I didn't want to burden you with my issues about Maggie.'

'I'd like to talk about her now, if that's alright?'

He nodded. 'Okay. I'll make us some tea and bring it through. You go and sit down—put your feet up.'

'Will you…erm…' she licked her lips and eyed that smattering of hair on his abdomen '…get dressed?'

He looked down at himself and then back at her, raising a sardonic eyebrow. Then he smiled and nodded. ''Course.'

Callie waited for him in the lounge while he disappeared off to his room. Soon enough he came back through—dressed, thankfully, in jeans and a white tee. He moved into the kitchen and came back with a tray of tea and a small plate of biscuits.

'Hungry?'

Definitely. But not for food…

'I couldn't eat.'

'I could make you an omelette?'

She shook her head. 'This is fine. I'll eat properly later.'

Callie inhaled a deep breath. She wasn't sure she wanted to hear some of the answers, but there were questions and she had to ask them.

'So tell me about you and Maggie.'

'What do you need to know?'

'What went wrong?'

He shook his head as if he didn't know himself. 'We should never have married. Plain and simple.' He shook his head, disgusted with himself. 'I was stupid. On the rebound. When we first got together, everything seemed fine. Or I pretended it was, I guess. I was so determined to make it work with her, and love her, and give her anything she wanted to make her happy.'

On the rebound? 'So what went wrong?'

He shrugged. 'I really thought I loved her. I thought I was proving it to her every day. She seemed happy, for a few years, at least, but then she started looking at me strangely and asking me weird questions.'

'Like what?'

'Questions about you. Us. Our friendship. There was a distance coming between us and I panicked. I didn't know what to do. I knew she felt that there was something missing, and when she mentioned children I was determined to give her the child that she wanted.'

'But that didn't happen.'

'She learnt she couldn't have children. When we couldn't conceive the distance between us became greater. Because of her infertility, I believed. She was so sad, and I so wanted to make her happy. When you suggested the surrogacy I leapt at the idea.'

'*You?* Not both of you?'

He shook his head. 'Not at first. But I persuaded her it was a good idea. She had doubts, but she agreed to let us look into it. When she started to have counselling at the infertility centre...that was when it all started to go wrong.' He took a sip of his tea. 'There were issues in our relationship from the start. I truly believed I loved her, and she insisted that I didn't. But that wasn't true. I *did* love her...in a way...just not in the way I should have.'

Callie nodded in understanding, sad that he'd never confided in her about this before. 'When I worked with Maggie on the ward she kept questioning me about the surrogacy. About my feelings about it. My feelings for you.'

Lucas looked at her. 'Did she? What did you say?'

'That of course I was happy to do it. That I loved you. That I couldn't imagine not giving you the greatest gift a friend could give. She looked so sad.'

'It's hard to work in Maternity and then discover you can't have what's in front of you all day long...' He shook his head. 'I felt so sorry for her.'

'Perhaps you shouldn't have?'

Lucas nodded. 'I know. She told me the night she left that my pity was so obviously just for *her*, not for us as a couple. That I was truly showing her I wasn't connected to her in the way I should have been.'

Callie felt sick. Why hadn't he confided in her about all of this? She could have helped them both! Given them space, distance, time. Whatever it was they'd needed.

'And then she had her affair?'

'Yes. She told me she'd found love in the arms of someone who put her first for once. That she'd found someone who was willing to treat her right.'

'But you *did* treat her right.'

'No. I didn't.' He looked at her and smiled sadly. 'I thought I had. I truly did. But she was right about me, and I feel terrible for treating her in such a way. I know now that I'll never do that again. It's all my fault.'

He slid over to the couch she was sitting on and put his arm around her shoulders.

Callie sank into him. 'But it *wasn't* your fault! She should have said something! She had a voice. You were trying to make the best of what you had. You acted with good intentions—'

'I so wanted to put it right. In all of this I was trying to prove something. To myself, to my parents, to Maggie. I should have been thinking of you, and I want to put that right too.'

'You haven't hurt me, Lucas,' she said gently.

'I never want to—'

Callie heard the crack in his voice. Her heart swelled with concern and she hated the fact that he was hurting over what he might have done to her. She turned to hold him, comforting him, hoping her arms around him would convince him of her forgiveness. She kissed the side of his face, his cheek, his jaw.

Her lips were moving ever closer to his mouth and he pulled back, looking at her, searching her face with his eyes. 'Callie, don't do this if you're going to stop me again—'

But she leaned in and closed her eyes as his lips brushed hers. A fire ignited within her and she didn't fight it this time. This time she welcomed it, falling into his arms, falling into his strong embrace.

He kissed her as if the world was going to end, and when he stopped she was gasping for breath.

'I should have been stronger. I shouldn't have allowed you to be dragged into my mess.'

'But we're working it out, aren't we?'

He stroked her hair back from her face. 'Yes. But I need you to know, Callie.' He held her hands in his. 'I will never hurt you. I will never lie to you. I will be here for you, always.'

She had to blink back tears at his words. 'I still have doubts.'

'Why?'

'Because…because you've never had a relationship work out! At school, at college. Plenty of girls, plenty of dates, but never a commitment. And then with Maggie…even that was wrong…even that failed.'

'But I was so young then! You can't hold relationships I had at sixteen against me? They were all wrong for me. And I've just *told* you about Maggie…'

'And the others?'

He looked at her, his face a mask. 'I was a teenager. A young teenager. Hardly anyone has successful relationships at that age. Besides…the one woman I truly wanted turned me down.'

Callie stared, his words echoing in her skull, accusing her, blaming her. Asking why she had turned him down? She'd told him why! Did he not realise? Understand? Did he truly not appreciate just how much he meant to her?

He leant back against the chair and sighed. 'You should hate me,' he said quietly.

'But I don't. You can't take all the responsibility here,

Lucas. We went into this process with our eyes open. So you knew things weren't great between you and Maggie and you didn't say? Well, what about what *I* knew? What *Maggie* knew?'

'What do you mean?'

'You weren't the only one in that relationship—she knew how bad it was, too. She was even sleeping with someone else, for goodness' sake! And I was her husband's best friend and she still allowed me to get pregnant with a baby when she was messing around with someone else! You didn't do that.'

Lucas lifted her hands in his and kissed them, his lips caressing the backs of her fingers with a tenderness that broke her heart. 'We were all in the wrong. I'm sorry. With all my heart, I'm so sorry.'

'Don't be. Because you're *you*. Because you're truthful. Without this situation I would never have had a baby. I would never have been able to consider the possibility that I'm able to be a mum. I would never have tried to be. And I can only contemplate it because you'll be at my side. There are no doubts in my mind about what a committed father *you'll* be.' She stroked his jaw. 'You're nothing like your own father.'

'You'll be here with us?'

His eyes lit up with hope, and the realisation that he wanted her to be there so much almost broke her heart.

It was terrifying to say it, but she knew in her heart that she could. 'I'll try. If you want me to be.'

'I want nothing more than for you to try. Because I'm living my life for *me* now. Not for Maggie. No one else. Me. And this baby.'

As they sat next to each other Callie circled the few hairs in the middle of his forearms. 'I love it that we can be honest with each other.'

'Me too.'

'I don't regret the surrogacy, Lucas. I knew then and I know now that you're going to be the best dad in the world to this baby.'

She looked deep into his heart and saw that her words meant the world to him.

They decided to paint over the pale blue with a pale green, so that they could paint a jungle mural on the upper parts of the wall: tree foliage, brown monkeys hanging down from the branches holding bright yellow bananas, snakes with red and blue stripes wrapped around tree trunks, a bright yellow sunshine in one corner and some red macaw parrots flying from one side of the room to the other.

It was an ambitious project, but Callie had agreed to it after seeing Lucas's draft drawings. He was a pretty good artist and could sketch what he wanted to perfection.

'You weren't kidding about having an inner interior designer, were you?' Callie laughed. 'I don't suppose you've got an inner chef, too?' She was starving.

She was wearing an old shirt of Lucas's, tied in a knot below her bump, with some old jeans. He wore an old tee shirt with jeans and both of them were pretty much covered in paint. They'd been working hard on the room for hours.

The nursery was really beginning to take shape and Callie could picture herself there, holding the baby. She could imagine looking down and feeling something. Love, devotion... That bond that had always been missing from her daydreams before.

Everything seemed to be coming together. It was all starting to look rosy.

Lucas flicked some paint on her. 'Hey—planet Earth to Callie?'

She looked at him and smiled. Could a man look more delicious, wearing scummy old painting clothes with a smear of green paint across his forehead? 'What?'

'I said I've made arrangements for us to visit the castle. Didn't you say you wanted to go?'

Windsor Castle was one of the oldest castles in Britain, and it still stood in its entirety in the centre of London. Queen Victoria had gone there on her honeymoon with Prince Albert. The pictures she'd seen of the inside on the internet made the place look so romantic—like a real life fairytale castle, right in the heart of the capital. People could hire it out for celebrations, and last year couples had started getting married there.

'That's great! When?'

'After the next scan. I thought we could go as a treat— before the baby's born. I'm not sure we want to negotiate turrets with a baby buggy in tow.'

No. Those turrets looked narrow.

'That's great! Oh, I can't wait! I was always asking my mum to take me and she never did, and then one day at school we were all given a letter to take home about a school trip they were organising to go there.'

He listened intently. 'I think I know what's coming.'

She nodded. 'You're right. She gave me two pounds for the deposit, which I paid, finally thinking I'd get to go on a school trip, but then she never paid the rest. I stayed at school, doing algebra and factoring equations, whilst everyone else had a lovely time.'

'Oh, Callie…'

'My classmates came back full of it. Since then I've always meant to go, but when you live in the heart of somewhere you tend not to go to the touristy places.'

He put down his paint and held both her arms, looking her straight in the eyes. 'Well, we're going. After the scan to check the placenta we are most definitely going to the castle.'

She smiled at him, and this time she hoped he would kiss her. She wanted it to happen. If he did she wouldn't fight him or step away. Not today. Today she deserved to be kissed.

Lucas didn't disappoint her. He pulled her closer and dipped his head to hers.

Callie closed her eyes in expectation. This felt so natural to her now, and she wanted him so much! She'd denied herself years ago and kept Lucas stored in a box marked 'friend' for too long. She wanted his lips on her, his hands touching her, caressing her. She wanted to feel the love that he could give. To have that release. Just once.

As their lips met sparks flew. A barrage of sensations ripped through her body. It was like waking up after centuries of being asleep—every nerve-ending was alive and just waiting for him to caress it.

His hands cupped her face as their lips made sweet music and she inhaled him as if he were her only life's breath. Tenderly and slowly he removed her clothes, as if he expected her to stop him at any moment. He didn't rush her, but moved at her pace.

Callie helped him pull off his tee shirt to reveal his broad, muscular chest and she ran her hands over parts of him she had never seen, as if privileged now to do so. He was so perfect—so right. A delight to look at and to touch.

Briefly she wondered why she had denied herself this for so long. She wasn't thinking about what she was risking any more. Somehow she'd pushed those worries to one side, as if she was allowing herself this one night. Those thoughts were too burdensome, too disappointing, to let them rule her head now.

Her heart was in charge and she wanted Lucas. Hadn't they both wanted each other for too long? Well, dammit, this time it was going to happen!

Callie's fingers undid his jeans and they dropped to the floor. Lucas scooped her up to take her to his bed. This room smelt of fresh paint and they didn't want any distractions.

She laid her head against his chest as he cradled her to him before gently lying her down on the bed, lowering himself onto her, holding his weight off her round belly.

'You're so beautiful, Callie,' he murmured, kissing her skin in feather-light touches, trailing his lips down her body to envelop her peaked nipples. 'If you're going to stop me, then do it now.'

She gasped at the sensation, gripping his back, hungry for more. More than anything she wanted him inside her… To feel him filling her, to enjoy that ultimate surrender…

She wasn't going to stop him. Not today. Not any more.

He took her gently, but still she cried out his name. He stopped briefly to check she was okay and then he was moving. Rhythmically. His mouth claiming hers. Her body was his to control and she cried out in ecstasy as he brought her to her peak.

Her hands gripping his back, pulling him tighter against her, she went with him on his own journey to climax. When he finally collapsed above her, spent and sweating slightly, he kissed her once again and then just held her, as if she was the most precious thing he'd ever owned.

Callie kissed him back and he fell asleep in her arms.

CHAPTER SEVEN

It took Callie a while to fall asleep, and when she did she dreamt in fits and starts. Dramatic, terrible dreams in which she was on a small boat out at sea in rough weather. High waves kept crashing down into the boat and all she had was a small delicate china teacup to bail out the water. Just when she thought the boat was safe from sinking another wave would crash down, or she'd notice shark fins in the water and the music from *Jaws* would inexplicably be heard.

In the dream, her panic was rising and rising, and then in the distance, beyond the high waves, she spotted another boat—a larger, stronger boat. Lucas was aboard, with all his sisters, and they were waving and calling at her to come to them. But no matter how hard she rowed her stomach would start to hurt and she would have to stop.

When the biggest wave of all came crashing down upon her head Callie woke with a start and sat up, gasping, her eyes taking in the familiar room. She was safe and on dry ground. Beside her, Lucas slept peacefully, his face relaxed, his hair tousled and gorgeous.

Thank God for that. Just a dream...

She ached in places she'd never ached before, and she remembered last night and how Lucas had touched her... Why had she made them both wait for so long?

She wiped the sleep from her eyes and ran her fingers through her hair. Glancing at the clock, she saw it said six-thirty a.m. She had to be at work for eight a.m. Throwing back the covers, she went to swing her legs out of bed—but stopped when she saw all the blood.

'Oh, my God! *Lucas!*'

Lucas leapt up beside her. 'What is it?'

'You need to call an ambulance.'

'What?' Then he noticed the large pool of blood beneath her. 'Are you okay? Are you in pain?'

She hadn't thought so, but now that he asked she was aware of some cramping. 'A bit…'

Lucas leapt from the bed, pulling on his jeans and throwing his old painting tee shirt over his head. He grabbed his mobile from his jacket pocket and dialled 999. 'Ambulance, please.'

'What is the nature of your emergency?'

'My partner's bled overnight. She's twenty weeks pregnant.'

In both their minds they knew that twenty weeks was much too early for their baby to survive if he or she arrived now. They needed to remain calm, but it was hard.

'I need to put on some clothes.' Callie said, about to get up.

'No! I want you to lie still. I'll give you one of my tee shirts. Do nothing until the paramedics get here.'

'Am I losing it, Lucas? Am I going to lose the baby?' she asked in a timid voice. This was the most frightened she'd ever been in her life.

He came to sit beside her on the bed and laid his hand on her belly. 'We can't know. But you do know as well as I do that this can mean nothing. Just a breakthrough bleed.'

'But there's so much…'

Callie began to cry. What had they done? She knew they should never have done what they had—knew they should never have overstepped that mark. Look what had happened!

'Hey… Shh… Come on.' He leaned into her and put his arm around her. 'Have you felt the baby move?'

She thought for a moment. Had she felt anything since being awake? 'No—nothing.'

'That still doesn't mean anything.' But his face hardened, his mouth a bitter line.

It was the worst seven minutes of their lives, awaiting the ambulance. When the two guys in green made their way into the flat, carrying their big packs and smiling reassuringly at her, Callie couldn't help but burst into tears again. It was all so scary. She had no idea what was happening to her baby and wouldn't know until she got to hospital and got them to do a scan.

The paramedics were very kind, and they tried to keep her spirits up as they wrapped her in a cream blanket, strapped her into a portable chair and wheeled her down to their vehicle. In the ambulance they attached monitors and checked her blood pressure. It was a little low, but nothing significant that would indicate a major blood loss, which gave them a little hope.

Callie lay on the trolley after they'd transferred her over, concentrating like mad on her insides, hoping and waiting for baby to kick, to give her a sign that it was all right. That it was still there…that its heart was still beating.

Why won't you kick? You're always kicking me…

But she felt nothing, and by the time they wheeled her into the St Anne's Hospital, she was despondent and very upset. Convinced that because she'd slept with Lucas she had somehow killed her baby.

'This is my fault.'

'It's not.'

'I'm being punished, Lucas. It's because I never wanted to be a mother. It's life's cruel trick.'

'No, Callie, it's not. It's nothing to do with that.'

'How can you know? I never wanted to be a mum, and just when I manage to persuade myself I could be one life strikes a blow and takes the baby away anyway!'

'You don't know that.'

'The baby hasn't moved! And it's always kicking me. *Always.*'

Lucas felt helpless. And angry… Angry at the world. He knew what she'd be thinking. How she'd be blaming herself.

All he could do was hold her hand, when what he wanted to do, as a doctor himself, was take over and order a fast scan so that they could get the status of the baby. She hadn't continued to bleed, which was a good sign. The bleeding had happened overnight and then stopped for some reason.

But inside his rage was building. Rage at life playing cruel tricks. Finally he'd been allowed to have Callie and now they were being punished for it. He knew what she'd start to think. Start to believe. That their lovemaking was somehow to blame. That it had been wrong. He cursed the world for doing this to him. Letting him have a taste of her. A taste of what it could be like for them together. And then swiping it away before he could hold on.

The doctors took her blood pressure again and it had stabilised. They also brought a portable ultrasound machine to Callie's bedside.

Lucas took hold of Callie's hand and gripped it hard. He was trying to tell her through touch that he would protect her, that no matter what the result he was there for her and they would get through it.

The doctor added some gel to the transducer and slowly drew it over Callie's abdomen. It seemed to take an age, and then the doctor turned the screen for them to see.

There was a heartbeat.

'Oh, thank God!' Callie began to cry again, with relief,

and Lucas reached to embrace her and kiss away her tears 'So it's all right?'

'Baby's fine. Heart-rate is good—about one hundred and forty a minute, which is average.' He swirled the transducer around some more. 'Placenta is still in position—no sign of early abruption.'

Abruption would mean that the placenta was coming away from the uterine wall early.

'It's possible you had a breakthrough bleed—dramatic as it was. If it's okay with you I'd like to do an internal and just make sure the cervix isn't opening.'

Callie nodded. 'Check everything. I don't mind.'

She was happier now that she knew her baby was safe, and as if in response to her strong emotions the baby kicked.

She laughed. 'Ha! So *now* you start! You couldn't do that earlier?'

Lucas had felt the kick too and audibly exhaled, his own heart reassured that he wasn't about to lose the two most important people in his life.

'I'll call everyone—let them know it's okay.' By 'everyone' he meant his sisters and his mother, as he'd called them earlier from the ambulance, to notify them that they were on their way to hospital.

He left the cubicle, so Callie could have privacy for the examination, and used his phone.

Callie meanwhile was reassured to hear that her cervix was tightly closed, was not effaced or thinning out in any way, and that she was showing no signs of labour.

'There is a small spot of cervical erosion. That could have been the cause of the bleed.'

'Erosion? Right…' Lucas had been so gentle, though, and careful. Had she bled because she'd slept with him? Was this her punishment?

But of course it could just be 'one of those things'. Unfortunately for her, and everyone else who experienced it, 'one of those things' could be quite dramatic.

'Is it because the placenta was covering the cervix?'

The doctor seemed undecided. 'It hasn't yet moved up off the cervical opening, so it's a possibility, but with erosion we can't know for sure. It does look like it's recent.'

The doctor suggested that she stay on the maternity assessment ward for the day, just to make sure she had no further bleeds. It would also allow her to rest.

'You have a stressful job, Miss Taylor, and you said you were decorating the nursery. Perhaps you just overdid it a bit?'

She accepted the admonishment. She *had* been up and down the stepladder a lot. And she *had* made love with Lucas. What had she been thinking? A day of rest was probably a good idea. Though she felt a little embarrassed that her colleagues would have to look after *her* when they were overworked already.

They soon dismissed that silly idea. They were overjoyed to be looking after one of their own.

'It's so special!' one of them said.

Callie wanted Lucas to get some rest too, so she asked him to go home.

'No, I'll stay with you,' he insisted.

'No, Lucas. Go and get some rest. I mean it. I'm fine now, and everyone else will look after me. Please.'

She didn't tell him it was because she wanted him to go. She felt so guilty about having sex with him. As if they'd been punished for something they should never have done.

Would she have felt different today if there'd been no bleed? Possibly. But she *had* bled, and they *had* slept together, and it was clearly a sign that what had happened was wrong. It could never happen again.

Lucas did feel tired. So he agreed and kissed her good-

bye. Their lips lingered as they kissed each other, not wanting to part. But part they had to, and he stroked her face,
deep in thought, his fingertips tracing the soft curves of her
skin as if memorising the contours of her face.

She watched him go and closed her heart once again.

By the time he got back to his flat Lucas was exhausted. He
changed the sheets and then lay on his bed for ages, hoping
to sleep, but the last few hours kept running through his
mind. Hearing Callie's scream, the fear in her voice when
she'd called his name. Maybe on the outside he'd looked
calm, but inside he'd been a mess.

The fear of losing either of them had almost killed him
and the knowledge of that had made him realise something.

He loved Callie. Not just because she was carrying his
baby. Of course he cared for her because of that, but this
felt deeper. Something that had been awakened after a long
time. Something that had always been hidden there inside
him, but had masqueraded as his friendship with her.

Lucas loved being her friend—yes, he did—but…he
wanted more than friendship with her. He wanted to love
her properly, in the open, not just as friends but as lovers,
as a couple, as a committed partnership.

He'd seen her darkest days. He'd seen her go through so
much. And each time it had hurt him and he'd been there
for her—if only to hold her hand or to listen as she'd cried,
wept with despair or anger. They'd shared good times too.
Her getting into university, then qualifying as a midwife;
himself qualifying as a doctor.

They had a shared history. Had shared so much together.

Now they were having a baby.

Surely two people could not be connected more than to
have created a life together?

He got up and began to pace. Wanting Callie home.

Home.

They lived together. They were best friends. Were having a baby.

And he loved her.

But he knew she was afraid. Afraid of jeopardising their friendship. How could he make her see that she meant the world to him?

There had to be a way.

There had to.

Just thinking about her and the baby made him feel good, and his heart soared so high it might have been up in the stratosphere.

The baby meant so much to him. He loved it—he knew he did—that was without question.

I love Callie too. I do.

But could he have her in the way he wanted?

He needed to know that she would give him the commitment he needed. Not just to him but to the baby too. He'd lived his entire life wishing his own father would be more committed to him, rather than just being a disciplinarian and an occasional parent who swooped in from overseas for a week or two at a time…

Lucas needed to know that Callie would be there one hundred per cent. Not a weekend mother, not a godparent, not an 'aunt'.

A mother. A wife.

My first marriage might have been a dreadful mistake, but I could damn well be sure my second won't be.

He picked up his phone and dialled a number. A number he'd put into his phone just a few days ago. As it rang he hesitated, just for a moment, and wondered if he were doing the right thing. But then he thought of Callie and he just *knew*.

This was the right thing to do. But he'd keep it a secret for now. Surprise her.

As the phone was answered at the other end he grabbed his car keys and walked down to his car, making arrangements as he went.

He'd had a very productive evening with Sienna from the castle. Walking through the doors of the hospital the following afternoon, he felt less anxious. Hospital could be a frightening place for most, but for him, it almost felt like home. He liked working there—liked the people, the place. His work. He knew the team and he knew that Callie would be looked after well.

Upstairs in the maternity assessment suite Callie was sitting upright in bed and looking much better. There was colour to her cheeks and her face lit up when she saw him.

His relief at seeing her was overwhelming. 'Callie...' He kissed her and sat down in the chair beside her bed. 'How are you doing?'

'All right. I've had lunch, and the doctors say if I don't have any more bleeding in the next few hours I can come home.'

'That's fantastic.'

But he was looking about the ward, not looking at her. Distracted. Something had changed with him. What was it?

She looked at him, concerned at the odd tone in his voice. He didn't seem his normal self.

Something was wrong. Lucas was hiding something—she knew it. She could always spot someone lying to her or hiding something from her. She could smell a woman's perfume. She could also smell alcohol. On *Lucas*? What did that mean? Had he been drinking?

For some reason Callie chose not to say anything, but inside she hurt. Had Lucas been drowning his sorrows? Self-medicating with alcohol? Why would he turn to booze? She'd never known him to drink before.

She'd confront him later. Not here. Not in the hospital where they both worked.

'Did you get some sleep?'

'A bit.' He changed the subject. 'Have you spoken to your mum?'

Callie looked at him with a raised eyebrow. 'No. I figured because we're going to see her in a few days I could tell her then. If she's interested.'

'I'm sure she will be.' He squeezed her hand. 'Can I get you anything?'

The truth… 'You can get me out of here.'

He laughed. 'Soon. I *have* missed you, you know.'

Have you? 'I've only been gone a night.'

Lucas nodded. He knew that. They'd been the most unbearable few hours he'd ever spent.

Although Callie had her suspicions, she had to let them go for now—even if they *were* eating her alive. She would remain friendly until she had proof. She couldn't believe he was making her think like this! Making her suspicious. How *could* he? After all this time, after all her worrying about losing him as a friend, now he'd slept with her he'd gone out and celebrated, or something, and probably hadn't done so alone! That had to explain the perfume smell. The aroma of alcohol on him.

Why wouldn't he? He was a good-looking man. Charming. Women gravitated to him, didn't they?

She hoped her suspicions were wrong. Because if they were right then that meant Lucas was keeping things from her. *Lying to her.* She'd been lied to her whole life by the one person who shouldn't have. She couldn't do that again.

Not with him.

Not ever.

Lying was the worst kind of betrayal she could imagine.

* * *

They were just about to leave the hospital to go home, and were standing by the midwives' desk saying their good-byes, when the telephone rang. One of the midwives answered it, listened and then put her hand over the speaking part of the phone.

'Callie? I know you're not actually on duty, and you're going home, but it's someone called Rhea on the phone and she says it's urgent. She's been trying to call you on your mobile.'

Callie's mobile had been left at the flat. She reached over the counter for the phone while Lucas rolled his eyes in dismay. She shouldn't be working.

'Rhea, it's Callie. What's up?'

'You said I could call you any time, but I couldn't get hold of you on your mobile.'

'I left it at home. Is something wrong?'

'I've been having some pains. Tightenings, really. I don't know what to do.'

'Have you had a show or anything?'

A 'show' was part of the mucous plug that sealed the cervix, and it could sometimes be seen before labour started to show that the cervix was beginning to soften and dilate.

'No. I had a bath, though. It didn't help.'

'Well, are these tightenings strong? Are they painful?'

'More achey. A couple of them have taken my breath away.'

Callie thought for a moment. 'It could be Braxton Hicks, but you're very early on for them. Is the baby moving?'

'Like a trooper.'

'Well, that's good. It's up to you, Rhea. You can come in and let us monitor you for a bit—maybe run a trace to be safe—or you can stay at home and see what happens.'

'I think I want to come in.'

'Okay, you can do that.'

'Will you be there when I get there?'

Her heart sank. 'I'm sorry, Rhea, I'm on my way home now—you've just caught me. But the other midwives here will look after you just as well as I would.'

'But you *know* me. Know my situation.'

'I'll tell them.'

She got off the phone and explained the situation, and then she and Lucas headed home.

He was happy in the car, whistling or singing along to the radio. She couldn't be sure of what was going on, and she needed evidence before she confronted him. Besides, she felt so tired from the last twenty-four hours that she didn't want to ask.

When they got home she went straight to bed, on Lucas's orders, and fell fast asleep.

Lucas watched her sleep. He was glad he'd stripped the bed earlier and replaced the sheets with fresh ones. Callie looked as snug as a bug in a rug, her face relaxed and free of the worry lines she'd had over the last few days.

She'd seemed a bit odd in the car, and he'd thought about asking her if everything was all right, but he'd decided not to push her. He didn't want to hear that maybe she was having second thoughts about their having slept together.

That night had meant so much to him, and he loved her even more if that was possible. It had been a real fright to think that they might lose the baby, but everything had turned out fine in the end. Besides, if he started asking questions she might tell him what he didn't want to hear. Not now. He'd be giving her ample opportunity soon to declare her intentions. Fully. For the whole world to know.

Just thinking about that churned his stomach. Everything would change on that day. Either his world would fall apart or he would get everything he had ever wished for. And by arranging a surprise proposal at Windsor Castle he would know for sure whether Callie's commitment to them both was a hundred per cent. He didn't want a part-time parent for his child. He wanted a mother.

But he also wanted Callie for himself. As his wife. As he'd wanted her years ago. If she turned him down...? Well, he'd be devastated, but he'd survive. He'd done it once before and he supposed he could do it again. Though it would be harder this time.

But he couldn't see how she *could* turn him down. Weren't they perfect together? Hadn't they always been great together? And some of the best relationships came from being friends first... By being committed to each other they could know that they would always be together. As Callie wanted. She'd never lose him.

Unless she got cold feet.

What if she panicked? What if she backed off? What if the proposal scared her?

He was trying to arrange the perfect conditions, so that there wouldn't be a crowd to pressure her into saying yes. He wanted her honest answer. If she said yes it would be because she truly wanted to be with him—great—but if she said no...

Lucas tried to imagine hardening his heart. Being stoic at the disappointment. But he couldn't. It would just seem so devastating.

Was he ready to endanger himself like that? Was it worth the risk? What if she *did* say no?

It was like being on swings and roundabouts. One moment his heart was all for it, the next his need to protect himself swung into play.

But it's not just about me any more. This is about our child too!

He *had* to do right by his child.

His secret plans were starting to come together and he

could only hope she didn't suspect what he was doing—because he wanted it to be the biggest surprise of her life.

The stress that the bleed had caused both of them had been awful, and he knew she'd not been sleeping well lately. But as he sat looking at her now, the woman who was carrying his beloved child, he vowed not to lose her. To prove to her that they had a future together.

Lucas switched off the small bedside lamp and curled on to the side of the bed next to Callie. The last forty-eight hours had been awful. Terrifying. But they'd got through it—and they'd got through it stronger than they'd been before because they'd pulled together. It was what people did. People who loved each other.

A few days had passed since the bleed, and Callie and Lucas were sitting in Maria's lounge. Callie felt awkward. The strained atmosphere between her and Lucas had developed more and more, and once when he'd been in the shower his mobile had rung and she'd seen the name 'Sienna' when she'd looked to see who was calling.

Who was Sienna? Callie didn't know of anyone at the hospital with such a name, and she'd not heard him mention a patient called Sienna. None of his sisters or family was called Sienna, and it was hardly an *old* woman's name, was it? Sienna was a young woman's name. A *pretty* young woman's name. How did he know her? How involved were they?

She'd been tempted to look at the contacts list in his phone but had quickly put it down, not wanting to be that kind of woman who checked her partner's phone.

But then a text from the lovely Sienna had popped up. It had read: Fabulous! You're brilliant! Can't wait to meet again. Sienna xx

Her heart had been ripped in two. Had he cheated on her? The night she'd been in hospital?

Although grief-stricken at the thought of having lost him already, she'd pulled herself together, determined to get through the rest of her pregnancy with dignity. She would have this baby and give it to Lucas and then she'd walk away.

It was what she'd been going to do in the first place, wasn't it? Lucas and this Sienna woman could play happy families. It was nothing to do with *her*.

She must have been in a weird mood since, because Lucas had kept asking her if she was all right. She'd kept answering that she was 'fine', and now she had to get through this visit to her mother.

As Callie was having difficulty driving, and not feeling comfortable behind the wheel, she'd had to let Lucas bring her.

She hadn't been to her mother's home for years and, truth be told, the last time she'd seen it, it had been a bit of a dive. Clutter and rubbish had been piled up everywhere, as if she was a hoarder, with surfaces overflowing with empty cans and bottles. The odd plate of food mouldering. They'd had a massive row the last time Callie had been here.

The last time I was here I stormed out.

But now the flat looked totally different. It was clean...it was neat and tidy. The walls had been given a lick of paint—'Gareth did them...'—and the hallway had been freshly wallpapered. There were pictures of Maria and Gareth up in frames, and one of Callie as a baby in her cot had been given pride of place in the centre of the mantelpiece.

'The place looks great.'

Maria smiled, inordinately pleased that her daughter approved. 'We've worked hard to change it around. Money's tight, but it's amazing what a bit of spit and polish and a dozen or so bin-liners can do.'

Maria placed a tea tray on the low coffee table and poured them all drinks, offered round a plate of biscuits.

'I'm just sorry Gareth couldn't be here, but he got called to work on an emergency.'

'What does he do?' Lucas asked, thinking someone ought to show an interest, and Callie was oddly quiet. She'd been strange for days now, and he wondered if she suspected what he was up to. He hoped it *was* that. Because she was starting to pull away from him. The way Maggie had in the last few days of their marriage.

'He works for a counselling line. For ex-alcoholics. Because of his background he's got a lot of experience with helping people, and sometimes when they get a crisis call he goes in and helps out.'

'A counsellor? Wow…' So Gareth was used to helping out people in crisis? What had made him fall for Maria?

'Gareth is an alcoholic too,' Maria explained, seeing the question in Callie's eyes. 'But he's been on the wagon for twenty years. He still goes to AA meetings and that's where we met.'

'Two alcoholics together? Is that a good idea?' Callie asked.

'A lot of people may say two dependents living together is a recipe for disaster, but we don't think so. It's down to the individuals at the end of the day, and Gareth was determined to help me kick the sauce. And he did. Over six months now, Callie.'

She nodded. 'That's good, Mum. Long may it continue.'

Maria smiled, looking at both of them. 'It's a new start for me. Like this baby is for the pair of *you*. I'm so glad you two got it together in the end. I don't know why it didn't happen earlier.'

Callie and Lucas looked at each other. But it was awkward. Uncomfortable, somehow.

Lucas spoke. 'Things are complicated. We're taking it slow—not rushing into anything. We don't want to get it wrong.'

Callie rolled her eyes. It was twice now that Lucas had told people he and Callie were together, and each time she heard it she still felt scared by it. Did he still think everything was okay? There was a baby involved here—they couldn't afford to screw this up!

'How are you anyway, Callie?'

It was the first time Maria had shown concern for her and something inside Callie softened. She had to fight tears for a moment as the one thing she'd craved from her mother—attention and concern—was finally given.

'I'm all right. We had a little scare and I was in hospital for a few days, but I just needed to rest.'

'Oh…I do hope you're okay? Having a baby is a truly life-changing event—one that I got badly wrong. But I'm sure that you two will love this baby in a way I never could.' She turned to her daughter. 'I need to apologise to you, Callie. For everything. For the way I mistreated you. The way I put alcohol first. The way I neglected you. But it was a disease I couldn't fight at the time. Thank God for Lucas, here, because without him around as your friend I don't know how you might have turned out.'

'Wow…' She'd never expected an apology. She'd never expected this. 'Thanks… I guess I turned out all right…'

'All right? You're an amazing person, Callie, and I can't say enough how proud I am of you, and how sorry I am that alcohol took me away from you and stole the mother you deserved.'

Callie swallowed back tears. 'Well, thank you for the apology. It means a lot.'

The rest of the visit was spent with Maria showing Callie a scrapbook she'd managed to put together with scant pictures of Callie through her childhood and some of Maria and Gareth together. They spoke of the years of Callie's childhood, telling stories, sharing snippets of what they remembered.

There were lots of tears.

But there was lots of forgiveness and love too.

Callie got into Lucas's car for the drive home, feeling that bridges were now being forged that would hopefully never break. There was some hope for the future with her mother at last, but even though she'd made a good start today there were still many more days when it could all still go wrong.

Past experience had taught her that.

And present experience.

But she was hopeful.

And yet cautious.

I may be losing Lucas, but I'm getting my mother at last.

More weeks passed and Callie didn't have any more bleeding. But she made it quite clear that they would not be sleeping together again. She kept Lucas at arm's length.

Lucas understood her reticence and accepted it, though it was killing him not being able to touch her. He had even accepted her explanation of why, but he'd seen that she was being quite clipped with him, and sharp. He was beginning to fear that she was putting distance between them in time for the big day, so that she could still disappear and leave him holding the baby.

She was at thirty-four weeks' gestation and that day was getting closer. She had two more weeks left at work before she went on maternity leave. The nursery was all done and painted, a pram had been bought, and lots of tiny baby clothes in neutral colours. Lucas had bought some cuddly toys to go inside the cot which he'd spent the previous night building—with much swearing and cursing and dropping the Allen key constantly, or catching his knuckles on the wood.

The future was looking good for baby Gold, even though

he wasn't sure if Callie would be a part of it—and that broke his heart.

He knew he ought to be resigning himself to her leaving. All the signs pointed to it. His dad had been the same when he'd been at home and was about to leave again for foreign climes. He'd get sharp with everyone, snappy, find reasons for arguments. Callie was behaving the same way. Maggie had done it—why wouldn't Callie?

Everything was going really well pregnancy-wise. She'd even been receiving calls from her mother every week! Asking how she was and everything! Maria was certainly making an effort and trying to prove what she'd said to Callie.

'I'm going to be dry now, Callie. For ever. You can depend on me.'

'Wow. That's great, Mum. That would be amazing, in fact. But you've got to do it for yourself—not for anyone else.'

'I *will* do it for me. And for you. I know I wasn't the best mum in the world to you. I was no mum at all.'

Callie's eyes had welled up at that point and she'd found it difficult to speak.

Lucas had wanted to lay his hand on hers, to offer support, but that was difficult now. He knew Callie wouldn't appreciate it.

'Well, I'm behind you. You have my support. And I think I'd like to meet this Gareth who's made you like this.'

Maria let out a breath. 'I'd like to come and see you. When the baby's born. Perhaps I could bring him then?'

Callie had agreed. 'That'll be nice. I'd love that.'

When she'd told Lucas of the call he'd been just as shocked as she'd been, at first, but then he'd been so pleased! Especially when she'd mentioned that she'd invited Maria and Gareth to come after the baby was born. He'd picked her up and whirled her around the room, with her shrieking and squealing at him to put her down. How could he not know that it hurt for him to touch her and try and kiss her?

'Is everything okay?' he kept asking.

'It's fine. I'm just hormonal,' she'd reply.

When he wasn't looking she'd glance at him and feel sad. He'd let her down so badly. She'd not got an opportunity to look at his phone again for more messages from this Sienna person, but occasionally a text message would pop through and he'd look at it and smile before texting back.

Each time her heart would break a little more, and she'd dread when the time would come for them to part.

CHAPTER EIGHT

When Callie got into work the next day she was informed that her teenage patient, Rhea, had been admitted in early labour.

'She had a show last night, and then her waters broke this morning. She's in Room Two and she's waiting for you,' said Sarah, Callie's supervisor.

Callie was surprised. Rhea was at the same gestation as she was—thirty-four weeks. That was six weeks earlier than expected. Not drastic—the baby would more than likely be fine, although depending on its condition when it was born they would decide whether it needed to go to the Special Care Baby Unit or not.

Premature labour in teenagers was common. More common than most people knew. Lots of people assumed that teenage mums were healthy because they were so young, and would easily be able to carry a pregnancy to term, but unfortunately statistics and evidence didn't bear that out.

Callie grabbed Rhea's notes, quickly skimmed through them and saw that she'd been four centimetres dilated at her last check, which her colleague Donna had done only twenty minutes ago. Rhea had had a good night, had managed to get some sleep and was not using any medication—not even gas and air just yet.

She headed on down the corridor and got to the door of

Room Two. She tapped on the door gently and then popped her head in. 'Hiya—it's me. Can I come in?'

She was shocked to see a woman seated in the corner of the room, writing in a file. Who was *she*?

But Rhea was sitting on the bed in a beautiful red nightshirt and pink bed socks, one ear plugged into an iPod. She pulled the earphone out and smiled when she saw Callie.

'Thank God you're here! I was beginning to wonder if you'd ever make it.'

'I had no idea you'd come in.'

'I came in first thing.'

'Well, I only discovered that about twenty minutes ago. How are you doing?'

'All right. They don't hurt too bad at the moment.'

Callie nodded, then turned to the woman who was now smiling at her. 'Hi. I'm Callie, and I've been looking after Rhea throughout her pregnancy.'

The woman smiled politely. 'I'm Jessica. I'm the social worker assigned to Rhea's case.' She indicated Callie's bump. 'You look ready to have one yourself.'

Callie ran a hand over her burgeoning bump. 'Six weeks left. Looks like Rhea's going to beat me to it.'

'You can't stop babies when they decide to come, can you?'

Callie smiled. 'You certainly can't.'

Callie went over to Rhea and began to prepare the CTG machine. 'We need to run a trace for a little while. About thirty minutes. Is that okay? It's just with you having gone into labour early we need to make sure baby's okay.'

Rhea nodded and lifted herself so that Callie could get the straps behind her before applying the sensors to her abdomen and strapping them tightly. The baby's heartbeat was registering in the one hundred and thirties and the lower sensor measured the contractions.

She gave Rhea a push-button device. 'Record any move-ments you feel, okay?'

Rhea nodded, looking nervous.

'Don't be scared. This is all normal.'

'I bet *you'll* be scared when it's your turn.'

She laughed and smiled in sympathy. 'I probably will. And they always say medical personnel make the worst patients. I'll probably be a nightmare for whichever poor soul has to look after me.'

Rhea smiled nervously. 'What if I can't do this?' she asked in a small, terrified voice.

Callie sat herself down on the side of Rhea's bed. 'You? Not do this? Rhea? The brave girl who faced me off in her booking visit? What you've been through makes you the strongest girl in the world. You're here, you're a survivor, and you can and will do this.' She patted Rhea's hand, but Rhea grasped it, and Callie could feel her nerves. 'It's okay.'

Rhea met her gaze and nodded. But there were tears in Rhea's eyes.

'Look, I have to go and fill in your notes and then get Lucas. So I'm going to leave you for a bit whilst we get the trace. Try to use the time to relax. You'll need all your strength later. Can you do that for me?'

Her patient nodded.

'Put your head back, listen to some music, close your eyes. We'll be back in a jiffy.'

She quietly left the room, sighing deeply. Her own stress was building on Rhea's behalf. The time for her delivery was getting closer. Time for her to make a choice about her baby. They should have had more time. Another six weeks to get her to see that there were other options open to her. But time had been taken from them all. Was Rhea going to give her baby over to Social Services?

Sitting at the midwives' desk, she was writing up the notes when she felt Lucas's hand come over her shoulder.

She froze. Lucas had continued to try and touch her these last few weeks. It was baffling. Their relationship was seemingly just the same to him. Had he not noticed that she was trying to break away? So that when they did part her heart would remain in one piece?

She shrugged off his hand. 'Rhea Cartwright is here. Remember her? She's gone into early labour. Waters have broken, she's four centimetres, and she's in Room Two as scared as anything.'

'Don't you want to be with her?'

She nodded. 'She's got a social worker in there. I think she's going to take the baby if Rhea sticks with her decision. But whilst she's on the trace I thought I'd give her a break, you know?'

He looked at her, curiously. 'Give *her* a break or *yourself* a break?'

'How do you mean?'

'Well, I know how you feel about her case. Her giving the baby away. It has to resonate with you—it was what I was asking you to do.'

'But for completely different reasons. I hadn't been through what she'd been through.'

'So it would have been less traumatic for you to give away a baby because you hadn't been raped? Come on— you know that's not true. It would have been hard and difficult and heart-breaking, no matter what the circumstances.'

Callie rubbed her belly, feeling their child move and tumble around. There was less room inside now, so she felt every little stretch, every little movement, every little hiccup. It still could be heart-breaking. She had no idea if she would try to keep the baby herself now or give it to Lucas. She would most probably be giving it away. Unable to keep it or even be in its life.

Best not to think about that right now.

Was Rhea still okay about giving her baby away? Or was

she getting attached? Having doubts? Did she feel pressured to give up her baby because Jessica was in the room with her?

'I need to get her out.'

'Who?'

'The social worker. I need time to talk to Rhea.'

I may not be able to keep my baby, but Rhea could still keep hers.

'You can't persuade her to keep it, you know. That's not your decision.'

'I know, but I at least need to know that she's looked at all her options.'

'So what do you want to do?'

She looked to him for back-up. 'Come with me. Into her room. We'll say we're about to do an internal, or something, send her for coffee—anything to get her out of the room. I need to know that Rhea has thought through *everything* before she gives that baby away.'

Lucas breathed in deeply through his nose, thinking hard. 'Okay.'

They headed into Rhea's room and managed to persuade Jessica to go for a coffee whilst they ran some tests and examinations. Callie sat once more on Rhea's bed whilst Lucas stood by the CTG, looking at the trace.

'Hello, Dr Gold.'

Lucas smiled back at her. 'Hi.'

'Rhea, I'd like to talk to you,' said Callie.

'What about?'

'Your decision. About what happens after the baby has been born.'

'Oh.' Rhea looked down at her lap, fiddling with her earphones.

'Have you had any more thoughts about what you want to do?'

Rhea shrugged. 'I don't know.'

Callie didn't understand. 'You don't know? Whether to give it up?'

When Rhea looked up her eyes were full of tears. 'I don't know what to do! I was doing fine to start with. I was going to give it away—end of story. You know what I was like.'

Callie nodded.

'But then you bloody well made me see the scan! In 3D! I saw her *face*! Her sweet face… And you know what it made me think? That she *didn't* look evil. That she *didn't* look like a monster. It'd been so easy to think that she was.'

'Easier to separate yourself from it?'

Rhea nodded and sniffed. 'Yeah. But by then I'd got *them* involved, hadn't I? The Social.' Rhea wiped at her eyes with the back of her hand, then was gently handed a tissue from the box by Lucas. Rhea took it and blew her nose, wiping her face clean. 'I don't know what to do.'

She looked at Callie.

'How did *you* know you wanted to be a mother?'

Callie knew that was too long a story to go into. And if she was truthful about her own doubts that wouldn't help Rhea with hers.

She glanced at Lucas. 'I don't know… I guess it happened quite slowly. I had to get my head around the idea. It was frightening.'

'You were scared? But you're a midwife.'

'Worst patients, remember? I don't want to be flippant. It's an individual decision. But I think you know if you want to be a mother deep in your heart. Sometimes you think that you don't—that it'll be too hard, or it'll be too painful—but that's just a reflex reaction. It's not until you think about it…and I mean *really* think about it…that you know for sure. What's in your heart, Rhea?'

A contraction hit then.

They waited whilst Rhea breathed through it, and when she was done she let out a huge breath. 'Whoa! I think…I think I might like to try. When I imagine her life, lost in the system…'

Callie looked at Lucas hopefully. This was the sign she'd been after.

Rhea had another contraction then. A painful one.

Callie and Lucas looked at the CTG and saw that it was strong, lasting a lot longer than the others—nearly a full minute.

Callie got the Entonox ready and asked her if she wanted it for the next one?

'Are they all going to be like that?'

She smiled. 'They might get worse.'

'Then give it to me.'

Rhea took the tube and mouthpiece and waited, and another contraction came hurtling along, only thirty seconds since the last one.

Lucas looked at Callie. 'Things are moving on?'

She nodded. 'Definitely.' A glance at the clock told her that technically there were still two more hours to go before Rhea needed to be checked internally once again, but if she continued to have contractions that quickly, and for that length, they might not have them.

Rhea groaned. 'Here comes another one!'

She started breathing on the mouthpiece and Callie laid a hand on Rhea's stomach to feel the contraction. It was strong. *Very* strong. Rhea was gasping and panicking now, rolling around on the bed.

Lucas glanced at Callie, then whispered, 'What you said just now…about knowing in your heart whether you want to be a mother…'

She looked uncertainly at him. 'Yes?'

'Don't *you* know?'

Callie was saved by a knock at the door and Jessica was there, poking her head in. Callie asked her to wait outside for a moment. 'She's just about to have an examination…'

Jessica happily stepped back into the waiting room.

Callie asked Rhea if she could do an internal to check her progress.

Rhea nodded, and Callie began her examination to feel for the cervix.

But that wasn't what she reached first.

There was part of the umbilical cord visible.

'Prolapsed cord!' she stated.

Lucas quickly hit the emergency button. An alarm sounded and the bed was tilted backwards.

Callie warned Rhea that she was going to have to keep her hand inside her to keep the baby's head off the cervix.

'What?'

'You've got a prolapsed cord—we're going to have to take you to Theatre and do a Caesarean section.'

'Why?' Rhea began to cry.

'If the baby's head presses on the cord it'll cut off the blood supply and oxygen. I need to support the head and keep you tilted back so that gravity will help until we get you into the operating room!'

'But, Callie...'

There was no time for more conversation.

Other midwives came pouring into the room, along with maternity support workers and any paediatricians who'd happened to be present on the ward at the time. The general rule on Maternity was that if an alarm bell sounded you responded—no matter *who* you were!

They raced Rhea through the corridors, past a confused and shocked Jessica. Callie called out to her, to try and explain what was happening, but they were going past her so fast there wasn't time to check whether she understood what was happening.

Rhea was crying and gasping and trying to fight another contraction. 'Callie, what's going to happen?'

'We're going to give you a general anaesthetic.'

'Can't I stay awake?'

'I'm sorry, Rhea, it's an emergency.'

'But I want to *see* her! Don't let her take her away!'

She meant Jessica.

Callie nodded her understanding quickly and promised Rhea. 'No matter what, I won't let anyone take your daughter—not until you've seen her first.'

'And I hold her first. No one else gets to do that.'

Callie nodded. 'No one,' she agreed.

The anaesthetist quickly got a general anaesthetic into Rhea, and inserted an artificial airway to keep her breathing properly during the operation. Callie still knelt on the bed, holding the baby off the cord. She ached and hurt, and her belly was being kicked and punched from the inside by her own baby. All she wanted to do was sit back and relax and breathe a sigh of relief, but she knew she had to stay there until the baby was lifted out by C-section.

Lucas was scrubbing up, along with another consultant, and it wasn't long before he strode into the theatre. They made their incision, the seconds ticking away as they cut through the layers, burst her bag of water and lifted out the baby.

Rhea's daughter screamed her head off indignantly at being brought out into the very brightly lit room. She continued to cry until she'd been thoroughly wrapped in blankets and a towel and had her hair dried. Only then did she settle and go to sleep.

Callie climbed off the bed and went to the station where the paediatricians were working to see how the baby was getting on. Her knees hurt. Her lower abdomen ached from the position she'd had to be in. But none of that mattered. Rhea's baby was fine—only needing a little bit of oxygen to assist with her breathing. She looked a good size too: maybe even four or five pounds already. She didn't expect her to stay in SCBU for long. Not if she had the same determination and grit as her mother.

Lucas peered over at her. 'Is she okay?'

'Doing well.'

'And you?'

She turned and beamed a big smile at him. 'Fine.'

His eyes crinkled in the corners and she knew he was smiling back, even if she couldn't see it.

She informed the SCBU nurses that Rhea had insisted that Social Services were not allowed to see or touch the baby before Rhea had done so first.

'Social Services are around, and I don't know how pushy they'll be, but Mum gave strict instructions,' Lucas said, and Callie was glad and proud that he'd insisted on Rhea's wishes for her as well. He knew how important it was to Rhea.

'Don't worry—we'll look after her,' one of the nurses replied.

Callie discarded her gloves and washed her hands. Then she went to see Jessica.

'Everything's fine. Rhea's doing well—as is the baby.'

Jessica smiled and nodded. 'That's wonderful.'

'Rhea will be asleep for some time. She's insisted that she wants to see and hold her baby first. You won't be able to see her until she has.'

'I thought Rhea didn't want to see the baby?'

'It's Rhea's wish. She changed her mind and made it quite clear,' Lucas stepped in. 'We have to honour the wishes of the mother.' *As should you,* he wanted to add.

Callie went to get a drink, and had just made herself a cup of tea when Lucas joined her in the staffroom.

'Rhea's in Recovery. Doing well.'

'Excellent. I almost can't believe she's had her baby. We were going to be in it together until the end.'

She rubbed her stomach, aware that this was her last

few weeks of being pregnant. Would she ever experience being pregnant again? Was this going to be her only baby?

Crikey, I'm thinking too far ahead, here!

Lucas cocked his head. 'What's the joke?'

'Nothing. Just thinking about these last few weeks. Only six more weeks of being pregnant. It's scary.'

She chose not to mention all the other terrifying things. Losing him...

'Because you know all the things that can go wrong?'

'Because it's something I denied myself, not even considering it for so long. Now it's nearly at an end and I'm not sure how I feel about it. Whether I really *can* do it.'

He frowned. 'Be a mum? I thought you'd got your head round that?'

'What if I've been kidding myself? I'm good at doing that. What if this *doesn't* work out?'

'Why wouldn't it? So what if you get things wrong? Mothers do that all the time. So do fathers. But they carry on because they know that no one is a perfect parent, and that no one can do parenting without making mistakes.'

'Why are you so knowledgeable? You seem to know what you're talking about.'

'Because I believe in you. If you didn't care then you would have something to worry about—but you *do* care and so you don't. If that makes sense.'

She could see the pulse throbbing in his neck. He was clenching and unclenching his jaw. What she wouldn't give to touch him once more. Feel his lips on hers. The physical ache of longing for him almost knocked her off her feet.

'So, what are you going to do with your morning off tomorrow? Put your feet up? Knit bootees?'

She sighed. 'I thought I'd go into town. One last look around before I'm burdened with a buggy and have to hope people will hold doors open for me.'

He laughed and offered her a biscuit from the packet

on the table. 'Shall I meet you in town? I could be free around lunchtime? Maybe we could make it over to Windsor Castle?'

His face was flushed and she looked at him oddly. Why did he seem uncomfortable mentioning that place? Had he been there before? With this Sienna person? Maybe he'd met *her* there?

Maybe she *should* meet him tomorrow. There were a few things they needed to discuss. Time had not given her any answers. Any explanations. And it would be good to be on neutral ground.

'I'll meet you at the coffee shop opposite Laurie Park.'

She munched down four more of the biscuits before realising they weren't hers. They were *so* yummy.

'Oh, God,' she said, changing the subject. 'I'll buy some tomorrow. Replace the packet.'

'They're mine. Don't worry.'

But she *did* worry. She worried a lot.

Rhea was soon sufficiently awake and well enough to be wheeled down to SCBU. Lucas and Callie went with her.

They had to wait for someone to let them in, and then they manoeuvred Rhea round to the unit that contained her baby.

Baby Girl Cartwright.
Born: 2.37 p.m.
Weight: 4 pounds, 13 ounces.

'She's a good size,' Rhea said, peering through the plastic. 'Can I touch her?'

'How about holding her?'

The SCBU nurse got Rhea's daughter out of the unit and laid her in her mother's arms.

Rhea's face was a picture. It was a delightful mix of love and confusion and fear and excitement. And hope.

Rhea ducked her head to inhale her daughter's scent and examined her thin fingers and tiny nails. 'So little. So perfect.'

'And totally healthy for her gestation,' the SCBU nurse said. 'She's only here until we can be satisfied her oxygen levels are being maintained without assistance.'

'What is she on?' asked Callie, wanting to know the amount of oxygen assistance. The lower the number, the better.

'Only ten per cent.'

'That's good, Rhea. She won't be here long at all.'

Rhea smiled, but couldn't take her eyes off her daughter.

Callie reached out and touched the baby's cheek, wondering if *her* baby looked like this inside her. 'She looks like you.'

'She does. She's…beautiful. How could I ever have thought she was a monster?'

'You don't have to make any decisions you don't want to, Rhea. You can change your mind. You can ask for time. Social Services will hold off until you're ready to make a firm decision.'

Rhea's face darkened. 'I already told them, though. That I wanted to give her up.'

'But that was before. This is now.'

Rhea looked up from her daughter's face. 'But I'm on their radar now. Won't they think I'm a bad mother for wanting to give her up?'

'Of course not!'

Lucas knelt down in front of them. 'Have you thought about a name for her?'

Rhea looked shy. 'I thought of some. After the scan, when I knew she was a girl, I played around with a few names—you know, just in case.'

'No matter what path you choose for her, you can still name her,' Callie said.

Rhea smiled. 'Yeah? Okay. Then her name's Rosie. Rosie May Cartwright.'

Lucas smiled. 'That's beautiful. She's clearly a Rosie.'

'We'll leave you alone with her for a while. Let us know when you want to go back to the ward,' said Callie.

Rhea nodded.

Callie and Lucas walked away, standing at a distance in the corridor beyond the room where Rhea and Rosie were.

Looking through the window Callie saw all the other incubators, some covered with blankets to protect the babies' eyes from the overhead lights, and all the tiny babies—the ones fighting for life, the ones so small they were almost transparent. She saw the parents beside them, the fear on their faces, the grit and determination in the furrow of their brows that their babies *would* get better. She hoped that they'd all have positive outcomes for their stories. Unlike her.

'Look at them, Lucas. We're so lucky not to be in there. It must be horrible for some of them.'

He put a reassuring arm around her shoulders and she wanted to shrug him off. 'A lot of them will have been prepared for it. But you're right. And we shouldn't have to worry about coming here. Our baby is happy and well.' He reached over to rub her stomach and felt a reassuring kick in response. 'See?'

'Rhea's got a big decision to make. I hope she makes the right one. For her *and* for her daughter.'

'What do you think she'll do?'

'I honestly don't know. But I do know she's finally con-nected with her. It's what she needed to do. She needed to see that what she was giving away wasn't evil. I wish her well. I wish her happiness in whatever she decides, and I'll support her. She knows that.'

'And you know that I'm here for *you*, don't you?'

He turned Callie's face with his finger on her chin and made her face him. Looking into his blue eyes, she knew that she could never get tired of looking at them. They were a vibrant blue, like the down of a kingfisher as it sat above the water. The glint of sunshine was always reflected in them, no matter where he was.

'You've been odd with me ever since the bleed and I need to know, Callie, if you're here for the long haul or not? If you can't be—if you have any doubts—then tell me now, so I can be prepared. It's all of you or nothing. No half measures.'

She had to say something. Now was the time.

So she was blunt. 'I don't trust you,' she said, as simply as that.

Her doubts about him overwhelmed her. She couldn't stand it anymore! Keeping up this pretence, this façade that everything was okay and hunky-dory. She *had* to know if he'd lied to her! She needed to ask him. Because they couldn't move forward unless he told her the whole truth.

There could be no other way for them.

'Have you lied to me, Lucas?' She turned to face him, a whole yard of empty space between them. Her stomach was churning in anticipation of his answer. Would he try to lie even more to get himself off the hook?

'What?' Lucas looked shocked at her question.

'Did you *lie* to me?' Her voice rose slightly and she saw him glance around to see who might be listening.

'No!'

He sounded angry. With himself…?

But she could *see* the lie in his eyes, and the knowledge that he was keeping something from her broke her heart. She physically felt the pain in her chest.

'You have, haven't you?'

'No, Callie!'

'And now you're lying about lying! That's what happens when people tell untruths. They twist themselves into knots and show those around them that they have no respect for them!'

'I respect you more than anyone!'

'But not enough to tell me the truth? Why not, Lucas? Is it because you're afraid to tell me? You haven't been honest with me. I thought you cared for me…I thought…I began to believe I was good enough for you!'

'You are—'

'No! I'm *not* good enough for you because you've lied to me. Easily, it seems. My mother did that. I wasn't good enough for her to bother about and she lied to me. Every single day. Do you know how that feels? To be worthless?'

'I have *not* lied to you! And if we're going to play the blame game, what about you?'

'What *about* me?'

'You know I needed one hundred per cent commitment from you—but could you give it? Ever? You blow hot and cold, like a bloody kettle, and I never know where I stand from one moment to the next! One day you want to be a mother—another day you doubt it. You let me sleep with you one minute, then push me away the next.'

'You're blaming *me*?'

'Well, who else is there?'

She laughed harshly. '*You*! You and bloody Maggie, for getting me into this mess in the first place. If you hadn't been so keen to prove your marriage to yourself none of this would have happened!'

'None of this would have happened if you'd said yes to me in the first place!'

She stared at him. What he'd said… Was that true? Had him asking her out all those years ago truly meant something to him? She'd thought he'd asked because he'd been out with most of the girls he knew and she was the only one left!

He shook his head, upset, and then something came into his eyes. Knowledge. Knowledge of what she was talking about—about his keeping something from her. He tried to hide it.

'All these weeks you've been off with me…I thought it was because you've had second thoughts about us sleeping together…'

'Oh, I have. I regret it completely!'

'Callie—'

'I never thought that *you* would lie to me. *Ever!*'

'Callie, it's not what you think—'

'No? You came to the hospital stinking of booze and perfume! There were strange messages on your phone! Who's Sienna?'

His face blanched white. 'She—'

'No! I don't want to hear it! I can't bear to look at you right now…leave me alone!'

She turned from him and began to run away, back to SCBU. Lucas called her name, then ran down the corridor to grab her arm.

She shook him off. 'Leave me alone, Lucas!'

People were looking, watching them, so Lucas hung back, his jaw clenching, frustrated with himself for answering her with a knee-jerk reaction and saying he hadn't lied. He knew he should have told her the truth.

I will *tell her the truth. I'll tell her the truth and make her listen to me.*

Rhea waved at Callie through the glass to come in and she entered slowly, taking in the lovely sight of mother and daughter. 'Are you ready to go back?' she asked, and sniffed, determined not to show Rhea that she was upset.

'I've made a decision.'

'Yes?' Callie's heart was in her mouth. Whatever Rhea decided she would back her one hundred per cent, but there *was* one direction she was hoping Rhea would take more than any other.

'I'm keeping her. Even though I have nothing. No equipment. Nothing. I'm keeping her.'

Callie gasped with delighted surprise, letting out all the pent-up breath she'd not known she was holding. Then she was smiling and laying an arm around Rhea's shoulder, hugging her, trying her hardest not to cry even more.

'Well done. I'm so pleased for you! Do you want me to tell Social Services?'

'No, it's all right. I'll do it. They need to hear the truth from me.'

'I'm sure it'll be fine. They can still help you.'

'I hope so. My daughter is going to know her family. Be loved. That's what matters at the end of the day, isn't it?' Rhea looked up at Callie.

She nodded.

Yes it was.

More than anything.

Callie hadn't come home. He'd waited and waited, but there'd been no sign of her. He'd called her phone, but it either kept ringing or was switched off. He'd thought about going round to her mother's to see if she was there, but anger had stopped him.

Why was he so cross?

Okay, so he'd kept a secret—but it was a small secret, and it was one worth keeping for the surprise it would cause. It was a *good* omission of truth. He couldn't tell her he was going to propose!

And what had she done? Overreacted. That was what.

Instantly blamed him, not giving him a chance to explain himself, and then running off like...like someone in a dramatic movie.

Well, this wasn't a movie—this was real life. And he was mad at being tarred with the same brush as her mother.

One tiny mistake. Just one. That was all he'd made, and now Callie was using that to punish him for someone else's mistakes.

It was more proof to him that she couldn't commit the way he needed her to. Was she so frightened of commitment that when she actually had the chance of it she threw it away? Was she unable to recognise just what he'd been about to do for her?

There was no other way he could prove his commitment to her. Apart from being there every day. And he couldn't prove that ahead of time until he was actually doing it! But by proposing marriage, by showing her that he wanted that commitment from her...

He loved her! Plain and simple. That was how it had always been with him. But after that time she'd pushed him away he'd been cautious about showing it. Yes, there had been girlfriends at school. But he'd been so young! There had even been Maggie. But that had all been a façade to hide the fact that there was only one true love that he'd always wanted and craved.

Callie.

And she was unable to see it.

Why couldn't he make her see it?

Lucas lay in his bed and stared at the ceiling. Sleep wasn't coming easily.

By morning he was exhausted, and desperate to talk to her, but he had to go to work. He'd been paged with an emergency and had no time to try and find her. Hopefully she'd call later, because he *had* to get this sorted with her. He had to know whether she wanted to be with him or not.

Because he wouldn't lay his heart on the line a third time.

CHAPTER NINE

THERE WAS A book in her bag and Callie began to read as she waited, but she was so tense and nervous none of the words would go in. She kept reading and re-reading the same passage over and over again, until she gave the book up as a bad job and put it away again.

She was just closing the zip on her bag when the doorbell sounded as someone entered the café and she looked up, hoping to see Lucas, but it wasn't him.

She wondered if he'd remember that they were supposed to meet today in this little coffee shop opposite Laurie Park.

He probably wouldn't arrive. Not after their argument. She'd run out on him and not gone home, instead getting a taxi and going to her *mother's*, for crying out loud!

When had her mother ever been there to support her? Never. And yet…the world had gone topsy-turvy. Lucas had lied and let her down and the one person who'd never been there for her suddenly was. Life was screwed up and she couldn't possibly see how it would ever right itself.

She missed him like crazy. This was her most dreaded situation. To have lost Lucas. To have lost her best friend. Her pillar. Her rock. Her heart. She would give him his baby and then leave and go…where?

She wrapped her hand protectively around her baby, her feelings torn.

Where did you go when your heart was torn in two? Was there a place that could heal that? She didn't think so.

Her coffee sat untouched and cold on the table and she stared at her phone. Perhaps she could ring him? He was meant to be at home, unless he'd been called in to work, so he should answer. Perhaps she should hear his explanation? Though she couldn't imagine how he'd wriggle out of this one!

But she'd dialled his number without thinking.

He didn't answer for ages. She could imagine him standing in the hospital corridor, or at home, his hand rubbing at his eyes, pacing the floor, staring at nothing as he focused on the terrible question she'd posed.

Was he going to answer? It was taking him a long time…

'Callie?'

'Lucas.'

'Where are you? You didn't come home last night.'

'I stayed with my mum, but I'm at the coffee shop now.'

There was a pause. 'Of course. We were meant to meet there today. Before we went to Windsor Castle.'

She nodded, hearing the sadness in his voice.

'I don't know how this went so wrong. I want it all back to how it was before.'

'You mean before you lied to me, Lucas? You had an affair—'

'An *affair*? Hang on—what are you talking about?'

She closed her eyes in despair that he could still be trying to wriggle out of it. 'I know about Sienna.'

A shocked pause. His silence spoke volumes.

'You do?'

'I saw her message on your phone. The day after you came to me in the hospital, stinking of alcohol and her perfume.' Her voice broke and she hiccupped back a sob. She was *not* going to let him hear her cry.

'Oh, Callie, you've got it all so wrong!'

'I don't think so…'

'Callie, listen to me. I am not having an affair with Sienna! I was planning to propose to you! At Windsor Castle. She's the events manager there and she arranged for us to have a private part of the castle opened just for us so I could ask you to marry me! She served me champagne— that was why you could smell alcohol on me!'

What? A proposal? To *her*? To Callie?

'I was meant to be proposing to you today, Callie! At the castle! I was going to meet you at the coffee shop and then suggest we go for a walk around, only to surprise you!'

'But—'

'Everyone else knew about it! My family, your mother— they were all going to be there. But I had to cancel because I thought you'd fallen out with me.'

Oh, no!

Could it all be true? Her mother had kept trying to get her to call Lucas, but Callie had ignored her…

The baby gave Callie a hard kick to her bladder and she held her stomach, gasping… She felt sick. To her very core. She dropped her mobile. It began to ring again and she could see it was Lucas, but…

The whooshing noise in her ears was getting louder and she leant against the table as the world began to grow dark.

'I…'

She'd leapt to conclusions. Terrible conclusions. Because that was what she was used to! People letting her down. Lying to her. Treating her like a fool. And she'd accused him of having an affair…

She'd been so wrong. How could she have got it so wrong? She should have trusted him, given him the chance to explain… He'd promised he would always be truthful to her…

Her face grew hot and as she lifted up her hand to wipe at her forehead she stumbled forward, hoping to go outside to get some fresh air. But her legs were weak and jelly-like, and before she knew it she'd gone crashing down in the café, smacking her head violently on one of the tables.

Lucas was suturing in Theatre when the internal phone rang. A theatre assistant answered it, and Lucas expected it to be a quick reminder from his lead consultant about their meeting that afternoon. He really wasn't in the mood for it and he didn't want to go. All he could think about was that call from Callie.

Callie had rung off and then hadn't answered his calls. The urge to go and find her and right the wrong of having lied to her was strong, because he knew how she felt about liars. Her own mother had lied to her throughout her life and it was something she couldn't tolerate. He knew that.

I should have told her the truth from the beginning.

But he'd been trying to protect her and had thought a little white lie wouldn't hurt. How wrong he'd been! And now he hadn't been able to get away. There'd been emergency after emergency in Maternity that day. He was hoping for a break after he'd finished up here, so that he could grab a coffee and try and see if Callie would answer her phone yet.

When the assistant brought the handset of the phone over to him and held it to his ear he got a call he'd never expected.

'Dr Gold?'

'Yes? Who is this?'

'My name's Dr Alan Carter. I'm an emergency doctor down in A&E.'

'Yes?' Perhaps he had a maternity emergency down there and wanted some advice?

'We've had a patient brought in, thirty-four weeks, who's received a serious blow to the head and abdomen. There's internal bleeding and we need to deliver.'

'Right. I'm just finishing up in Theatre…'

'The ID in her bag states her as being Callie Taylor, and you're the ICE number on her phone.'

The ICE number was an 'In Case of Emergency' number that police officers liked everyone to have on their phones in the event of situations such as these.

'Oh, my God…how is she?'

'She's currently unconscious. We're having her rushed to Theatre Two now.'

'The baby?'

'We have to deliver the baby or she could bleed out. The trauma has caused a heavy bleed and we've had to rush her in for an emergency section.'

Lucas stared at the needle and suture in his hand. Two more stitches and he could be gone. But he didn't have time for two more stitches. He looked up at his foundation year one doctor and passed him the tools. 'Finish off.'

He ripped the mask and scrubs from himself, flinging on new ones and scrubbing his hands clean, then dashed from the department and hurtled down the stairs, not bothering with the lift. The doors banged as he slammed them open and raced down the long corridor. Staff and patients stared in wonder. It had been maybe five minutes since the call.

Lucas grabbed a nurse—any nurse who was walking by—and explained who he was. 'Callie Taylor. In surgery. Where?'

She seemed to look him up and down, saw his ID tag, noted he was an actual doctor and not just some weirdo off the street and pointed down towards where the emergency theatres were. 'But you can't go in!'

'Try and stop me.'

He pushed past her but was stopped at the security doors. There was a viewing window, and he planted both hands on the glass like a prisoner and stared through.

He could see Callie. Well, her head, anyway. One eye was swollen and starting to blacken and her other eye was taped over. She had a tube down her throat, helping her to breathe. An anaesthetist sat by her head, measuring all her responses and saturations, and by looking at the monitor Lucas could see she had very low blood pressure. Anything beyond that, he couldn't see.

The surgeons were beyond a green scrub screen, but he could see a baby monitor in the corner, manned by two women, and there was a flurry of theatre staff, all doing various things, concentrating hard on their patient.

There was a speaker button by the glass and he pressed it. 'I'm Dr Gold. The patient is my partner. How is she?'

The surgeon turned and peered at Lucas over his mask. 'She's in a bad shape, but we're doing our best.'

'How's the baby?'

'We're just about in. We'll let you know in a moment or two.'

It was an agony of waiting. They seemed to be moving so slowly at times. There didn't appear to be any urgency and it was all he could do to fight the urge to get scrubbed up and go in there himself! But he knew, sensibly, that he'd be no use. In fact he'd be a gibbering wreck!

I can't lose them. I love them.

I love her too much to lose her! And I never got the opportunity to show her!

What if she died? What if he lost her now and he never got the chance to prove to her that he'd been committed to them working out?

There was a weak cry and Lucas looked up, hope flooding him. The baby! The baby had been born!

It was handed over to a nurse, who took it away into the far-off corner. The staff stood over it whilst they worked. Lucas could see them using suction and oxygen and towels to rub some life into it. But the baby looked floppy. Unresponsive.

No! No, come on, baby! Cry again! Cry! He jabbed the communication button hard. 'What's going on?'

'She's weak, but we've got a heart-rate,' the nurse said.

She? I have a daughter?

'And Callie?'

The surgeon didn't look at him. 'We're still working on her. If the bleeding doesn't stop wc may have to do an emergency hysterectomy.'

The baby let out a louder cry and Lucas exhaled heavily, slumping against the glass. He'd literally not been able to breathe and was winded now, as if he'd taken a sucker punch to the stomach. On shaky legs, he stood once again, just in time to see the baby wheeled out of Theatre.

He stopped them. 'Is she okay? I'm the father.'

She was a perfect pink bundle, wrapped up and swaddled in towels within a large incubator.

'She'll be okay. But she needs to be kept warm.'

'Where is she going? SCBU?'

They nodded and pushed past him. He let them go.

He was thrilled she was fine—thrilled to be a father finally, after all this time—but what mattered to him right now was Callie. He had to know she was all right. He had to be able to talk to her. To get a chance to put things right between them. He sensed they could have a great future together and he wanted to ask her something. To let her know that he would look after and love her always.

But it was awful to stand there and see her looking so lifeless and broken on the table.

But I will bear it. If she can, then so can I. Fight it, Callie. Fight it like mad.

He rested his forehead on the window and waited.

They fixed her skull and her womb before wheeling her through to recovery. He sat beside her bed, holding her hand and staring at her pale face, willing her to wake up.

Lucas kissed his beloved's fingers and reached over to kiss her face. 'Come back to me, Callie. Come back to me so I can tell you the truth. I love you. Do you hear me? I love you. We have a daughter who needs you. As do I.'

The machines continued to beep as Callie slept on. Her vital signs were good, he convinced himself of that, though he wondered how Callie might cope with a newborn *and* a bad head. It wouldn't be a problem the first two weeks, when he was at home, but he'd have to go back to work eventually… Perhaps he could get his sisters round to help? They loved babies. They'd fight each other for the opportunity.

He smiled and stroked Callie's hand. 'We're all waiting for you. And your daughter is waiting for you to hold her. She's waiting for her mum to name her, though if we could refrain from naming her after items in the room…' He laughed and felt tears as he recalled Callie's memory of how her mother had named her.

It would all be so different for their daughter. She was loved already. She was wanted. She would have a beautiful name and a beautiful mother.

And if Callie gave him the chance, then they could have a beautiful future together too.

After a few hours in Recovery, they decided to wheel Callie up to Maternity. The neurosurgeons had offered to visit her there, to monitor her, thinking she'd prefer to be by her daughter when she woke up.

Lucas had visited their baby briefly and put his hand through the little round window. His daughter had clutched his finger, breaking his heart and then swelling it to twice its size with love for her. She truly was a beautiful baby, and showed no signs of being harmed in the collapse—which was a miracle. She had dark hair that was quite thick, like Callie's, and when she'd briefly opened her eyes to squint at the world Lucas had seen they were a beautiful dark blue. Violet-blue, he thought to himself.

The staff had weighed her and discovered that she was six pounds four ounces—a good size for her gestation. The small birth-card read *'Baby Girl Taylor'*. He wanted to get that changed. He wanted to name her. Give her an identity. But he still *knew* her. Here was the little girl who had kicked him through Callie's abdomen, who had responded to his voice when he'd leant over Callie's belly and read her bedtime stories.

'I know you!' he'd whispered. 'Remember? *Fee-fie-fo-fum*!'

He'd not been there but a brief moment when he'd felt a gentle hand upon his shoulder. Expecting a nurse, he'd turned round, then smiled in surprise. 'Rhea! How are you? How's Rosie?'

'Doing well. They say she can go home soon. Is this yours? Is it Callie's?'

He'd looked back at their baby and nodded, unable to speak.

'She had a section, then?'

'Unexpectedly.' He couldn't say any more as his throat clogged with a lump.

'She'll make a great mum, Callie.'

'She will.'

'What are you calling her?'

He shrugged. 'We haven't decided. I said Callie could choose. To right a wrong from her past.'

Rhea frowned, not knowing what he meant, but she wasn't about to pry. 'Well, I'll probably be gone by the time she's come round. Will you thank her for me? Tell her how much I appreciate her? I got her this card.'

Rhea handed over a small pink envelope.

'Of course,' he said softly.

If she'll let me.

CHAPTER TEN

SLOWLY, SOUNDS AND sensations began to become clear. There was the beep of a heart-rate monitor and occasionally the cuff around her left arm would be inflated.

Measuring my blood pressure.

Hmm... Why's that?

And then, as she opened her one good eye and began to see the interior of a hospital room, she began to remember details.

She'd been at the coffee shop and then… Callie blinked and looked down. Her pregnancy bump was gone, though there was still some roundness, and by the side of her bed, fast asleep, sat Lucas, his hand still holding hers.

Where's the baby? Is it okay?

Her need to know about the baby made her speak.

'What's happened?'

Callie inhaled deeply through her nose. She could feel a small nasal cannula there that she hadn't noticed before. More and more sensation was coming through now. Looking at his sleeping face, so innocent, only made her feel like weeping. He'd lied to her, yes, but it hadn't been what she'd thought. Years of being messed about by her mother had made Callie instantly think the worst! But she'd been so wrong. So terribly wrong!

He mumbled slightly, then blinked slowly and looked up, his gorgeous blue eyes widening at the sight of her awake.

'Callie...'

'Where's the baby?'

He reached for her hand again and clasped it tightly, kissing her fingers. 'In SCBU. We have a daughter, Callie. A little girl. And she's beautiful, like you.'

Tears pricked at her eyes at the thought of a daughter. A baby girl! Oh, how differently she would do things! Her daughter would be loved and cherished and know deep in her soul that she was the most precious thing to her mummy.

I'm a mum...

'Callie, I'm so sorry I tried to keep the proposal a secret. I just wanted to show you how much I love you and want to be with you. For ever.' His eyes were dark and full of love. 'That you'll never lose me. That we'll always be together.'

He's never let me down in all the years I've known him.

'I do love you, Lucas...'

'And I love *you*—more than words can say. Can you trust me? Can you believe in me?'

She thought quickly, knowing in her heart what her answer was.

Yes... I can believe in you. I do believe in you.

'I'm so sorry!'

The pain lifted from her heart at her words. She reached out for him.

Lucas took her hands in his and leaned forward to kiss her.

She closed her eye, accepting the kiss. His lips touched hers so lightly it was as if he was afraid to kiss her harder in case she broke. She had to laugh, and then winced as a pain stretched across her stomach.

Of course. I must have had a Caesarean.

'Callie, I—'

'Shh. Don't talk. Let me speak. I'm sorry I got angry with you.'

'I'd never—'

'I know! I know. But back then… I should have trusted *myself* more. I'm so used to being lied to by people who are supposed to love me. When you told me about Sienna it was my fault I didn't give you chance to explain.' She sighed heavily. 'The fault was with me. I'm sorry. I should have trusted you more.'

'*I'm* sorry… We should never have secrets from each other. Planning the proposal the way I did, in secret, was a bad idea.'

Callie smoothed the hair on his head and cupped his face. 'It was a wonderful idea.' He was so gorgeous. So handsome. And he was all hers. Mind, body and soul. She knew that now. 'So…we have a daughter?'

He nodded, smiling, his eyes lighting up. 'She's gorgeous and she's absolutely fine. When you're stronger, we can go and see her.'

'I want to see her today. I need to hold her. Feel her in my arms.'

'I'll check with the nurses—see if we can arrange it.'

'I love you, Lucas Gold. But you're going to need to know that I may just love our daughter a bit more.'

He smiled. 'I can deal with that. But there's something *you* need to know too.'

'What?' she asked sleepily.

'I'll be damned if I'll have a baby with the woman I love and not marry her…spend the rest of my life with her.'

Callie smiled, her grin stretching her face. 'Are you asking me to marry you?'

He slipped from his chair and got onto one knee. 'I am. Calendar Taylor…I love you more than the world can ever know and I would be the proudest man alive if you would agree to be my wife.'

She nodded, smiling, her face aglow from happiness and the assurance of trust. 'I will.'

Lucas got up and kissed her again. Her mouth, her cheeks, her neck, her mouth again. 'You've made me so happy.'

'Me too.'

After that, she didn't remember much. The anaesthetic was still in her system and she must have fallen asleep again.

When she woke, some hours later, it was dark outside and Lucas still sat beside her bed. He reached into his pocket and pulled out a small box.

'I was going to give this to you when you went into labour, but seeing as you skipped that step...' He opened the small velvet-covered box to reveal a beautiful platinum ring, with sapphire stones set in an oval shape, surrounded by diamonds. Callie held up her left hand and let him slide the ring on. It was a bit small, so she had to put it on her little finger.

'Wait for the pregnancy fluid to disappear. It'll fit then,' she said.

'The nurses say if you give them the nod we can go and see Baby Girl Taylor.'

'Baby Girl Taylor-Gold,' she corrected.

'I like that.'

It was a bit of a squeeze, getting Callie's bed into SCBU, but they were used to adjusting the space for mothers in beds or wheelchairs who were eager to see their babies.

Lucas propped some pillows behind Callie's back so she could see into the incubator properly.

'Oh! She's amazing!'

Lucas looked through the little cot. 'Isn't she? Do you want to hold her?'

She looked at him. 'Have you?'

'No. I wanted her mother to be first.'

Callie smiled with happiness. 'What shall we call her?'

The SCBU nurses helped them open the incubator and they delicately laid their daughter in Callie's arms.

'You name her. I think it's only right.' Lucas held his daughter's foot, fingering her small toes as they peeked out of the blankets.

'She's so pretty.'

'I know. We make good-looking babies, me and you.'

Callie gazed at her daughter's face, seeing similarities with herself and Lucas. The eye-shape was all Callie, as was the nose, but she had her father's mouth and ears.

'So much hair, too... I'm so glad this worked out between us, Lucas, because I'm telling you now I don't think I'd ever have been able to give her away.'

He kissed Callie's cheek. 'You don't have to worry about that any more. You've given me a gift so wonderful I can never thank you enough.'

Face to face, they looked down at their daughter. Callie could feel the roughness of his stubble against her cheek and smell his familiar aroma, and she felt safe and secure, despite the fact that her head was throbbing and she had a wound across her stomach that would make bikini choices in years to come an interesting challenge.

'What do you think of Isabella?'

He nodded. He liked it. 'It's beautiful.'

'Isabella Marie.'

'After your mother?' He'd not expected that. But it was a measure of how much was changing now. Even Callie's mother had changed since meeting her new man.

'Isabella Marie Taylor-Gold. I love it. I love *you*.'

She smiled, and then bit her lip in surprise when Isabella opened her eyes and snuffled, her mouth opening as if searching for something. 'Do you think she wants a feed?'

He shrugged. 'You could try.'

'Her suck reflex might not be ready.'

'But the skin-to-skin will be good for her.'

Lucas helped Callie undo her hospital gown, so that she could lay Isabella inside her clothes, against her skin. Isabella seemed a lot happier and was soon rooting around, searching for the nipple.

'Amazing.'

Isabella managed a quick feed and then dropped off to sleep.

Callie just wanted to hold her for ever, and Lucas just *knew* he'd get to hold them both for ever. He would get to make Callie and his little girl the happiest people alive.

He'd prove it to them.

Every second of every day.

EPILOGUE

THEY PICKED A date in June for their wedding. They'd planned to get married as soon as possible, but Callie wanted the bruising gone from her face first. Then when they did enquire at the castle about dates, they had to wait another year to get the perfect summer wedding Callie dreamed of. Mother Nature smiled down on them with beautiful sunshine, warmth and birdsong. The little chapel in Windsor Castle was bedecked with white flowers, and the place was filled to capacity with family, friends and work colleagues.

Everyone was there to share in their happy day.

Callie walked down the aisle in a simple off-white dress, strapless, with a tight bodice and flowing skirt, and behind her toddled their daughter, just short of two years of age, assisted by Marie Taylor, her grandmother, who held the basket of rose petals that Isabella was tossing all over the chapel floor.

Lucas looked at them both as they entered through the archway and knew that he could never be happier. Coming towards him was the woman of his dreams, gliding along the floor, her hands holding a delicate posy of pink roses.

She looked gorgeous, and when Callie stood by his side he reached out to take her hand. He laughed with delight as Isabella took her place next to Callie and peeked out at her father from beyond Callie's skirts.

'Boo!' she said, making everyone laugh.

The vicar intoned her solemn words as the sunshine shone brightly through the stained glass windows and filled the chapel with bright light and blessing.

They turned to each other and said their own vows, staring deeply into each other's eyes. Callie's voice broke at the beginning, but she ended strongly. Lucas was the other way round. His vows rang out loud and true and steady, and then, as his thoughts focused on how he'd nearly lost her and Isabella once, he faltered. He had to take a breath, take a moment to gather himself, before continuing on in a quieter, but deeply determined voice.

No one had any objections to their marriage.

No one burst through the church door at the last minute to protest.

No one laughed or gasped at Callie's actual name.

They exchanged rings, held hands and looked deeply into each other's eyes. Callie wondered how she could be so lucky. If someone had told her a few years ago that she would be marrying a man with whom she had a daughter she would have laughed in their faces.

What? Me? Married? A mother? Don't make me laugh.

Yet here she was, and she was happy beyond imagining.

Lucas looked so handsome in his wedding suit—a dark charcoal-grey. He had matched her pink posy with a pale pink tie and pink rose buttonhole. As he looked down at her she could read every emotion in his face. Happiness, love, joy, devotion.

It was how it was meant to be, but there was one more secret she had to tell.

The vicar pronounced them husband and wife. When Lucas leaned in to kiss her Callie closed her eyes and allowed herself to sink into the bliss of their connection as their lips touched.

The congregation cheered and clapped, and after they'd signed the register they walked down the aisle together, this time as man and wife. They stood outside as confetti rained down upon them.

Isabella ran around their feet in delight at the cascade of fluttering paper in pink and yellow and white, scooping it off the floor and throwing it back into the air. Lucas bent down to pick her up, not knowing she still had a handful, and when he had her in his arms she let the confetti go above his head.

What could he do but kiss his beloved daughter and then his wife?

As the photographer snapped pictures Callie leaned in to her husband and began to whisper something.

He didn't quite catch it and had to ask her to repeat herself.

'I said, I'll be damned if I'm going to be married to you and only have *one* child.'

He hefted Isabella into a more comfortable position and frowned, his brow furrowed in an amused question. 'You want us to have another?'

Callie leaned in close and whispered in his ear. 'We already are.'

Lucas stared at her as the realisation sank in. Overjoyed, he leaned in and kissed her, passionately this time, as if he could consume her. The crowd of onlookers cheered and whistled.

When they broke for air he looked into her pale blue eyes and told her he loved her. 'More than words or actions could ever prove.'

'And I love *you*—and Isabella—and whoever is yet to come.'

He grinned and nodded his head at the crowd. 'Should we tell them?'

Callie shook her head. They were already sharing this wonderful day with the people they loved. This new secret was one she wanted to treasure for themselves just a little while longer. 'Soon.'

'All right. At least you're not sick yet.'

She laughed. 'Oh, yes. I must admit I'm not looking forward to *that* part again.'

But she didn't have to worry. This time her pregnancy didn't make her regret her decision. There was only a little nausea—no clutching of toilet bowls for Callie Taylor-Gold.

And when their baby boy, Benjamin, was born, seven months later, they knew their family and their happiness were finally complete.

* * * * *

MILLS & BOON®

Want to get more from Mills & Boon?

Here's what's available to you if you join the exclusive **Mills & Boon eBook Club** today:

✦ *Convenience – choose your books each month*
✦ *Exclusive – receive your books a month before anywhere else*
✦ *Flexibility – change your subscription at any time*
✦ *Variety – gain access to eBook-only series*
✦ *Value – subscriptions from just £1.99 a month*

So visit **www.millsandboon.co.uk/esubs** today to be a part of this exclusive eBook Club!

MILLS & BOON®

Need more New Year reading?

We've got just the thing for you!
We're giving you 10% off your next eBook or
paperback book purchase on the Mills & Boon
website. So hurry, visit the website today and type
SAVE10 in at the checkout for your exclusive

10% DISCOUNT

www.millsandboon.co.uk/save10

MILLS & BOON®

MEDICAL ROMANCE

THE ULTIMATE IN ROMANTIC MEDICAL DRAMA

A sneak peek at next month's titles...

In stores from 6th February 2015:

MILLS & BOON®

Why shop at millsandboon.co.uk?

Each year, thousands of romance readers find their perfect read at millsandboon.co.uk. That's because we're passionate about bringing you the very best romantic fiction. Here are some of the advantages of shopping at www.millsandboon.co.uk:

* **Get new books first**—you'll be able to buy your favourite books one month before they hit the shops

* **Get exclusive discounts**—you'll also be able to buy our specially created monthly collections, with up to 50% off the RRP

* **Find your favourite authors**—latest news, interviews and new releases for all your favourite authors and series on our website, plus ideas for what to try next

* **Join in**—once you've bought your favourite books, don't forget to register with us to rate, review and join in the discussions

Visit **www.millsandboon.co.uk**
for all this and more today!